THE ALIBI

"Thanks, Kate," the inspector replied. "I'll leave you to it and catch up with you when you've got all you can. Right now, I need to speak to his wife again."

"Good idea," Kate put in. "These affairs are usually domestic. Especially when kitchen knives are involved. Only the woman of the household would know where they are. Keep it in the family, eh?"

David grimaced. "I don't think so this time. I know her. And she'd need a long arm. She was in Paris at the time."

POINT CRIME

THE ALIBI

Malcolm Rose

■SCHOLASTIC

Scholastic Children's Books
Commonwealth House, 1–19 New Oxford Street,
London WC1A 1NU, UK
a division of Scholastic Ltd
London ~ New York ~ Toronto ~ Sydney ~ Auckland

First published by Scholastic Ltd, 1996

Copyright © Malcolm Rose, 1996

ISBN 0 590 13370 5

Typeset by TW Typesetting, Midsomer Norton, Avon
Printed by Cox & Wyman Ltd, Reading, Berks.

10 9 8 7 6 5 4 3 2 1

Prologue

The car cruised to a halt by the hedge that separated the Burrages' back garden from the quiet street. Convinced that no one was watching, the driver leapt from the car and squeezed into the secluded garden through the laurels. It was a hot July afternoon but the figure, in trousers, baggy coat and hood, seemed to be dressed for winter. Stealthily, the stranger crept past the swimming pool. Without wind, the water was perfectly still, making a brilliant mirror for the house and the blue sky. The dark shadow of the uninvited guest floated across the pool's calm surface. By the back door, the figure hesitated, looked round and listened for a second. The garden was not overlooked. The intrusion had gone unnoticed.

A steady hand emerged from the coat and reached for the back door. The handle yielded to pressure. The door was unlocked. As it opened, strains of a Mahler symphony filtered through. Under the hood, only the lips of the intruder were visible. They curved into a smile. Music would deaden the sound of the approach. Like an angel of death, the cloaked figure slipped into the kitchen and shut the door noiselessly. On the table, there was a warm teapot, sugar bowl and biscuit tin. From the rack, the hand selected the knife that felt just right. Cautiously, the prowler slid out of the kitchen and into the hall. The study door was ajar. Inside the room, Stuart Burrage was absorbed in working at his computer, his back to the door, bombarded from all sides with classical music.

Knife in hand, the killer sidled into the study and tiptoed towards the victim.

It was only when the blade came over his head and appeared suddenly at his throat that Stuart turned his head. Startled and petrified, he was unable to react or save himself from the swift application of the knife. He issued a short gasp and a stifled cry as he collapsed on to the floor.

The posture of his assailant, kneeling by the body but avoiding the blood, exuded satisfaction. It was a clean and professional killing. One hand pulled back the shirt sleeve on Stuart's left arm to reveal his old-fashioned watch. The other hand still held the knife. The murderer prepared to break the watch by smashing down the handle of the knife on it but hesitated, then stood up and examined the computer instead. Again, the lips under the hood smiled broadly. Deciding against damaging Stuart's watch, the intruder discarded the knife, and retreated quickly – into the hall, through the kitchen and out into the beautiful, peaceful summer day. In seconds, the culprit had disappeared behind the hedge, climbed into the hired car and, undetected, driven away from the carnage.

1

Sea horses, queen angelfish and sergeant majors glided slowly and aimlessly across the screen. Crabs crawled across the sandy bottom and bubbles rose regularly to the surface. Artificial gurglings issued from the computer. In the centre of the screen, the water appeared to have turned crimson. Unconcerned, the fish swam through it.

The bloodstain should have been deep brown but the glow of the screen saver illuminated it from behind, turning it bright red, like a thin ruby curtain caught in sunlight. The blood had cascaded down the screen and dripped on to the keyboard below where its true rusty colour showed against the function keys. It had seeped between the buttons and congealed, gluing them together. Between the mouse mat and table lamp, there was a full cup of cold tea and two biscuits.

Unnaturally white, Stuart Burrage's body lay on the floor by the computer desk. His throat cut while he used the computer, he had toppled off the chair and hardly moved. He had not even tried to crawl towards the telephone to summon help. The blade had been applied clinically and accurately. Death had come quickly. Near his body, the carpet did not show an obvious stain but the thick brown pile was heavily matted with blood.

The study was large and luxurious. There was an easy chair and a huge filing cabinet. One entire wall was given over to cluttered bookshelves. Most of the volumes were sturdy hardbacks. Many were reference books on law. A few family photographs, none older than five years, were also displayed on the shelves. The other three walls were decorated liberally with valuable modern art, a family tree, framed qualifications and a newspaper clipping bearing the headline "Surgeon Gets Life". Along with the leather-topped pedestal desk, there was an enormous antique clock, a cabinet containing expensive hi-fi equipment, two imposing speakers, and an ornate fireplace. The green lamps on the CD player and amplifier were still lit but the symphony had finished, the speakers dormant. The clock ticked rhythmically and its pendulum swung impressively but its weights were nearly touching the bottom of the case. For Stuart Burrage, time had already stopped.

His wife, Rhia, opened the front door and called into the house, "Stuart, darling? I'm back." She instructed the taxi driver to place her suitcase just inside the hall and paid him. Then she shut the door and, still wearing her elegant blue coat, headed for the study. From the doorway, she could see that the computer was on, but at first she did not see her husband. When she stepped further into the room, she spotted him slumped on the floor. She flung her handbag on to the armchair and dashed to his side. She did not need to check for a pulse. When she took his hand, it was leaden and cold. As she turned away, she noticed the kitchen knife under the chair. She buried her face in her hands and ran from the room.

Distraught and tense, Rhia sat in the lounge while the scene-of-the-crime team invaded the study. She had no wish to watch them going about their grisly job, like vultures picking over a carcass. The police officer in charge, Detective Inspector David Thompson, was a friend of the family. He tried to console Rhia and extract information at the same time. "I'm sorry, Rhia. It must be a terrible shock – and a terrible loss. He was a good man – and a great lawyer. I always respected Stuart. I enjoyed working with him." David Thompson had first encountered

Stuart three years ago when they were both involved in the same case. Subsequently, they had met socially and the detective had struck up a particular friendship with Rhia. Now, he touched her arm gently. "I've taken personal charge of the investigation. I'll get whoever did it," he promised.

"But it won't bring him back," she sobbed.

"No," he murmured. "I can't do that."

Rhia sniffed and wiped her face with a handkerchief. "You have to ask me some questions, I think. Can we get it over with?"

Sympathetically, David replied, "Yes, of course." He cleared his throat, sighed, and began, "When did you come back and find him like that?"

"I don't know exactly. I didn't call straight away. I couldn't ... you know."

The police officer nodded considerately. "How long do you think it was?"

"About half an hour, I suppose, before I felt up to calling."

"That's OK," he replied. "I understand." He glanced at his watch to confirm the time.

Rhia's eyes were inflamed and her natural grace had been eroded by grief. She looked haggard and dismayed.

"Where had you been?" David queried.

"France. Paris. I just got back."

"Business or pleasure?" he asked.

"A little break, that's all. Stuart might have come

as well but work got in the way – as always. Now I wish he had come," Rhia murmured.

"How long were you there?"

Rhia looked askance at him.

"I have to ask," he explained, "to establish the time of death. That's all. Presumably he was fine when you left. Between then and now…"

"Yes, I see," Rhia put in. "I went on Thursday. Four days. A long weekend really."

Seeing the family photograph on the mantel-piece, David was reminded of Rhia's stepson. He enquired, "Is Kieran around?"

"He's competing in Scotland. Swimming."

David asked, "When did *he* leave?"

"A few days before I went to Paris. He went with his girlfriend, Ali. She's a swimmer as well. They're due back on Wednesday."

"Ali? What's her other name?"

"Tankersley. Ali Tankersley." Rhia added, "She's a nice girl."

"Well," David concluded, "I'll need to talk to you some more, I'm afraid, but for now I need to attend to … the study. And you need a rest. I'll get one of my chaps to make a drink for you. OK?"

Detective Inspector Thompson stood in the door-way for a moment and surveyed the scene. Immediately, one of his sergeants started to update him. He listened and, at the same time, prowled round the room. He stopped by the framed news-paper clipping and studied it for a moment. Tapping it, he muttered, "The infamous John Evans case. A surgeon turning the knife on his wife. He got life for it. A young Stuart Burrage was the barrister for the prosecution." He turned to his colleague and said, "Jim, check Evans is still tucked up at Her Majesty's pleasure." He hesitated, then added, "And trace all Burrage's cases for anyone who might bear him a particular grudge. Maybe he prosecuted someone who was later shown to be innocent. That sort of thing."

"I've already got someone on it," the efficient sergeant responded with a satisfied smile.

"Good. What about entry?"

Jim stayed beside David as he continued his slow tour of the room. "Not forced," he answered. "Probably just walked in through the back door. It wasn't locked."

"Pity," he mused. "Footprints in the garden?"

"Ground too hard. And no obvious tyre marks in the road."

"OK," David said, sighing. "Check door-to-door in case the neighbours have seen any suspicious vehicles – or people – out the back." Stopping by one of the forensic team, he asked, "Any decent fingerprints?"

"Lots. Mostly the same, though. Still checking."

Arriving at the computer, David watched for a

while the fish swimming unconcerned through the polluted water. "Very calming," he remarked. "Didn't calm the attacker, though."

Jim inquired, "Do we turn it off and take it back for examination?"

"No," David replied urgently. "Certainly not. Best to examine it right here and now. Call in Kate. She's a computer buff. She'll relish this one. If it was left active in a document there'll be information about when he logged on and when he last edited it. That's probably when he died. Judging by the untouched tea, I'd say he'd just brewed it up, put on a CD, and sat down to work when he copped it. If we turn the computer off to take it away, we might not get back into it again. If he had a password to gain access, it would shut us out. Right now, it thinks he's still alive and working on it. Get Kate in quick. It'd just be our luck if we had a power cut."

"OK." Jim scuttled away.

Looking at the forensic pathologist kneeling by the body, David enquired, "Is it as obvious as it looks?"

"Yeah. Pretty professional slitting of the throat. Immediate loss of blood pressure, then massive drain into the carpet. Dead in seconds."

"When?"

The pathologist shrugged. "Still need more tests. Less than a week, more than thirty-six hours."

Frowning, David said, "Any ideas why his left

sleeve's pulled up but not his right?"

"No. I've checked his left arm. There's nothing untoward. Perhaps he was looking at his watch when he was attacked."

"Mmm. Keep me informed." Then he called, "Someone bag this knife for me. I want to show it to his wife. See if it's home-grown."

David resumed his circuit of the room, aloof from the comings and goings of his team. He stopped by the family tree. It told him little more than he already knew about the Burrage family. Kieran was the sole offspring from Stuart Burrage's first marriage. He was seventeen years of age. After the death of his first wife, Stuart had married Rhia Swithenby five years ago. Rhia was an only child and she had not had any children herself. Her only surviving relative, her father, had died last summer. "Someone's done a lot of work on this. It goes back a good few generations of Swithenbys and Burrages," David mumbled to himself. "Saves a question or two." Nothing else in the room caught his eye.

Every time that David worked with Kate, he thought that she was more manic and more of a genius. With the flamboyant gesture of a maestro settling in front of a grand piano for a concert performance, the white-haired forensic scientist drew up the chair and flexed her fingers theatrically.

"Let's see what we've got," she began. "I doubt if he was actually typing when he was attacked. Some blood would have run down his hands on to the keys. He was twisting round, perhaps, to see who was creeping up behind him. Then the blood spurted from the side of his neck on to the top of the screen." Extravagantly, she demonstrated the effect by twisting her neck to the side and tracing with her hand the path of the gush from vein to monitor. "He fell off his chair before it got too messy. Most of it's in the carpet. Brown – good colour scheme for this sort of occasion."

Ignoring her gruesome sense of humour, David leaned over her and said, "What about the computer itself?"

"Let's take a look." Kate pulled on her nylon gloves and then moved the mouse a mere milli-metre. Immediately the fish disappeared to reveal a document containing only a title and a few words. "It's Microsoft Word. The beginning of a report of some sort. But he'd hardly got started."

From behind her shoulder, David muttered, "Interesting. Look at the heading. *Re: Robert Tankersley*. Same surname as the son's girlfriend." He read aloud the start of the document. "It is with considerable regret that I have to report the…" He smiled ruefully. "Cut off in his prime."

"Not everyone leaves the culprit's name written in blood, you know."

"Shame," David retorted.

"Tankersley isn't your man," Kate deduced.

"Why not?"

"Because he wouldn't walk away from here leaving this clue. He would've deleted it," Kate answered.

"Maybe," David replied. "Or maybe he was in a panic – or at least in a hurry to get out. Or perhaps he doesn't know anything about computers."

Kate shrugged. "Bet you waste your time on him. Anyway," she continued, "let's see what other goodies Burrage left for us." She clicked on *Summary Info*, followed by *Statistics*. "He started this report at 3.21 in the afternoon of July the twenty-third. That was Saturday, wasn't it?"

"Yes," David replied.

"And this is the first version. He didn't save a longer document that someone else has partially deleted. What you've got is all there was. The computer's been churning away, it says, for 2,649 minutes. Let me think. That's ... forty-odd hours. It makes sense, doesn't it? It's 11.30 now, Monday. Almost two days later." Turning towards David, she concluded, "Your man died two days ago." She pointed to the cup of tea and uneaten biscuits and said, "He got himself settled with a cuppa, typed for a few seconds, didn't even live long enough to get a sip or nibble a Hobnob. Throat slit at twenty-five past three."

"More than likely," David responded cautiously, "but not necessarily. He could have opened the document and then got distracted. Did this and that, and then gone off to make the tea."

Kate frowned. "This is a professional man. A busy barrister. He'd work efficiently – no distractions. He'd make the drink and then start working. He wouldn't take a break as soon as he'd started a new document."

"Probably not," David admitted. "But I have to keep an open mind."

Kate laughed. "The proverbial open mind! Good excuse for not admitting the obvious. Bet you pathology confirms it, more or less." She took a good look at the cup of tea and commented, "See the brown ring at the top? That's scum – caused by a couple of days of evaporation."

"Can that be measured accurately so we can find out when he poured it out?"

Kate grinned. "No chance. The rate of evaporation depends on room temperature and atmospheric pressure. And there's so little loss that any measurement would be inaccurate *and* imprecise. Forget it. Believe me, the computer record's much more reliable."

"OK," David conceded. "But one thing seems sure. He was murdered in broad daylight. Interesting."

Kate turned her attention back to the keyboard

and monitor. "What else did he do that day?" Under *File*, three other documents were listed. In turn, she opened them. Two were business letters and one was a financial report on a bridge club. Stuart Burrage was identified as the Bridge Club's secretary and treasurer. All three documents had been created on the 22nd July, the day before he was murdered.

"Running a bridge club's no big deal," Kate quipped.

David Thompson did not approve of her joke. He was too close to the victim to be amused. He agreed with her sentiment, though. "Probably not relevant," he said, "but can you get me copies of all these things?"

"I've brought a gadget. Wonderful things, gadgets. I plug it in to this system," Kate replied, patting Stuart Burrage's computer as if it were a faithful dog, "and it'll copy everything on to optical memory cartridges. And I do mean everything. It'll find even the hidden and protected files. Like extracting every last tooth. I'll take all his floppies as well. By the time I've squeezed all the juice out of his machine," she said with relish, "you'll need to demolish a rain forest to cope with the paperwork. But before you leave me in peace to get on with it, let's just check something else. I still believe in the human touch – well, mine anyway. You see, I wonder if he used e-mail." She left the file and examined the program manager. "Here we are. He's got a mailbox. Look. The last e-mail message was to someone called Daniel Allgrove. He didn't keep a copy of it but he asked for a receipt. Allgrove read the message at 2.55, it says. Half an hour before Burrage was killed." Kate looked at David and remarked, "I think you've got yourself another line of enquiry."

"Thanks, Kate," David Thompson replied. "I'll leave you to it and catch up with you when you've got all you can. Right now, I need to speak to his wife again."

"Good idea," Kate put in. "These affairs are usually domestic. Especially when kitchen knives are involved. Only the woman of the household would know where they are. Keep it in the family, eh?"

David grimaced. "I don't think so this time. I know her. And she'd need a long arm. She was in Paris at the time."

"I'm sorry to have to show you this," David murmured to Rhia, "but I really need to have it identified." He produced a polythene bag containing a black-handled kitchen knife. The blade was sharp, about ten centimetres long. "Is it yours?"

"I saw it before – in the study. Yes," Rhia answered, "it's one of mine."

"Sure?"

She nodded. "I use it all the time. It should be in the rack on the kitchen wall." She sighed wearily.

"OK." He continued, "I'll have to bring in an officer to take your fingerprints. We need to eliminate them. If we have yours, we'll be able to find out if there are any others on the weapon, door knobs and so on. He'll leave a kit so Kieran can give us his prints as well. Same reason."

Rhia muttered, "Fine."

Changing his line of questioning, David asked, "Daniel Allgrove. Doesn't he work with Stuart?"

"Yes. Stuart's junior partner. And a member of the Bridge Club."

"Did they get on OK?"

Rhia thought about it for a moment then replied, "Most of the time, yes. Stuart complained sometimes that Daniel had ideas above his station. It's just ambition, of course. Even so, Stuart had to put him in his place sometimes. You know, gave him the dreary divorce cases. Youngsters have to start at the bottom to learn the trade."

"So," David prompted, "Allgrove might resent Stuart, would you say?"

"Doesn't every junior partner feel he's being held back, peeved not to get the high-profile cases?" Rhia started to weep again. She had realized that her own husband would become the subject of a high-profile case.

"Do you want me to contact Kieran? If you know

where he's staying, we can get him back straight away. He should be here. A bit of comfort for you."

Rhia nodded. Through her tears she stammered, "I suppose so." She wiped her cheeks again and remarked, "You know, Kieran and I have never really hit it off. I might as well be honest and admit it. He was close to his mother. He used to be close to Stuart as well but a little less, I guess, since I came along. Even so, he'll be upset. He admired his dad."

"I didn't know the first Mrs Burrage," David commented delicately. "What happened to her?"

"Breast cancer."

David nodded soberly. "I see."

He took a note of Kieran's address and organized for a counterpart in Edinburgh to go and break the bad news to him.

2

In the afternoon, the Intercity train from Edinburgh to Kings Cross lumbered round a bend at a rakish angle. Ali flopped to one side and her head lodged against Kieran's sizeable shoulder. Kieran hardly noticed. He was gazing out of the window, watching the ragged Northumberland coastline rush past. He felt queasy and strangely detached, as if the world around him had gone into overdrive, leaving him becalmed. A mere passenger. He was recalling a time when he was ten and confused. One night, instead of reading him a bedtime story, his mum sat on the edge of his bed, gently placed her hand on his chest, and talked about a lump that had appeared in her breast. Apparently, it had been there for a while but her own doctor told her that it was nothing to worry about. By the time that a specialist had corrected the diagnosis, it was too late. She tried to explain that there would be surgery and treatment but that one day soon she would die. Kieran was puzzled and angry. A little lump did not seem to be such a big deal. And surely modern medicine could deal with a stupid lump inside his mum. But it couldn't. For the next year, he watched his mum deteriorate and then die. It just wasn't fair.

The sea disappeared behind rocks. For no apparent reason, the train slowed and then stopped altogether.

The young Kieran knew that his dad was special because everyone told him so. He was becoming the barrister that everyone wanted on their side. Kieran was proud of his dad but the demands of a top-class lawyer and a top-class father were too much for one man. When his mum died, Kieran's life seemed to grind to a halt. His dad hired substitute mothers for a while so that he could continue his career without a guilty conscience and Kieran did not complain because his father was special. It would have been selfish to hamper his rise to the top.

His dad sued his mother's doctor for negligence. He won a sizeable settlement and Kieran discovered that a value could be placed on his mum's life. The compensation amounted to a third of a million pounds. That was the court's view of what she was worth. Kieran didn't want money. He wanted a mother.

With a slight jolt, the train began to move again. Within a few minutes, it was back to full speed and the countryside flew past once more.

At his precious Bridge Club, Kieran's dad met a woman called Rhia. Within weeks, she seemed to turn up at the house at all times – even first thing in the morning. Before long, his father was sitting on Kieran's bed, just where his mother had once sat, to explain that he was going to have a new mother. The barrister within his father presented a faultless case that night. All of the advantages were expressed logically and forcibly. The twelve-year-old Kieran had no defence to offer. After his dad left the bedroom, he cried till morning.

And so Rhia became one of the family. From the beginning, Kieran imagined her as a sultry stranger and gunslinger strolling importantly and mysteriously into town, shooting down everything that his real mother stood for. He could never bring himself to call her "Mum". At least Rhia was wise enough not to force the issue. "You're a big lad now," she said, trying to flatter him, "so why don't you just call me Rhia? It is my name after all."

Kieran had to admit that, at first, Rhia worked harder than he did himself to establish a relationship. Yet he resisted her approaches. She just wasn't *Mum*. She was nothing like Mum. She didn't smell right. She was an intruder. She was younger than Mum and very good-looking. Straight after the wedding she set about sprucing up everything. She spent a fortune on the house and herself. Kieran's mum didn't care about money. She cared only that the family was happy. Kieran watched disapprovingly as Rhia splashed out mostly on frills for herself. Worse, it was the compensation for his mum's life that she was using to make her own life cushy. If his dad had not held her in check, she would have frittered away the lot. Her meals were extravagant and perfect, as well. His mum's cooking was always a disaster. Meals prepared by his real mother were an ordeal and an endless source of banter. There were times when he could hardly eat the stuff for giggling. There was nothing funny about Rhia's food. Kieran was suspicious of her and he had remained suspicious of her to this day.

Sometimes, Kieran would be regarded as special as well. It was explained to him that a man of his father's stature and occupation would occasionally make enemies. When a particularly nasty case was going through the courts, Kieran was sometimes given a plain-clothes minder. As Kieran grew older, he began to question his dad's chosen profession. When he was defending the most obnoxious characters who were clearly as guilty as sin, his father regarded it as a matter of personal and professional pride to secure a not-guilty verdict or at worst a minor punishment. Over an immaculate meal, Kieran would thump the table and say, "But that man stole millions and you know it! He may have been a company director – and he used a computer rather than a sawn-off shotgun – but he was still a thief. And you got him off with almost nothing." His dad would smile in an almost patronizing way. "You don't understand, Kieran. There were mitigating circumstances. He was stressed at work – he was ill. And some legal technicalities came into it." Kieran shook his head. "In other words, you were cleverer than the other side – so he got away with it. Your arguments didn't reduce the crime, only the sentence. You get paid to win the case, not to find out the truth." It was then that his dad destroyed for ever his faith in the due processes of law. He replied, "Let's not get confused, Kieran. The court's there purely to enact the law. It's a court of law, not a court of justice."

Ali stirred, opened her eyes and clutched Kieran's arm. "All right?" she asked.

Kieran nodded. "I suppose so. I was just ... thinking."

"About your dad?"

"About lots. Mum, Dad, Rhia, crime."

Tentatively, Ali whispered, "What do you think happened? One of the crooks your dad put away got his own back?"

"I dare say that's what the police will check out, but..." He did not carry on.

"What?"

"It doesn't matter," Kieran replied. "Just that it's not the only possibility."

Ali looked at her boyfriend. He looked sad and wistful. She realized that he was grieving for more than his father. She squeezed his arm and murmured, "It'll turn out all right. Promise."

Kieran and Ali went to the same school but they only really took note of each other when their dads got together one night to discuss business at Kieran's house. After the meal, the two fathers retired to the study like men from a bygone age expecting cigars and brandy. Rhia and Ali's mother chatted together and so Kieran was forced to entertain Ali. They were both fifteen at the time. They talked about their common interest in swimming and played CDs. Suddenly more than distant members of the same school swimming team, they became friends. It was a couple of months later when they realized that they shared more than friendship. At school Ali watched as Kieran used his big frame, and his status among the boys, to rescue a bullied lad called Grant McFarlane. She was proud of him. Later, at a gala, Kieran watched as Ali's effortless, almost lazy, backstroke powered her to first place. He was proud of her. Recognizing the pleasure that they gained from one another, they became a couple. Even so, when they went out together, they were relaxed about it. In the playground, other kids embarked on wild relationships, declaring their undying love for each other, falling out weeks later, and stumbling into the next heated relationship. Kieran and Ali seemed to regard it as inevitable that they would grow apart sooner or later and so they never declared anything, did not expect anything, and kept clear of passion. Two years later, though, when all of their friends had dozens of broken partnerships in their wake, Kieran and Ali were still together. Still strong. They had fallen in love without noticing it. Neither of them would admit it, even though they both accepted that life apart was unthinkable.

"I bet the police come and see Dad," Ali groaned.

Kieran glanced at her and said, "I guess so. But you don't think..."

"No," Ali interjected. "At least, I don't think so. All I know is that two years ago they were as thick as thieves, your dad and mine." She hesitated and then added, "Perhaps thieves isn't the best term to apply to a lawyer. Anyway, in the last couple of weeks, your dad's name's been struck off polite conversation at home. Some falling out! I even felt like keeping quiet about it whenever we went out together – as if Burrage is a dirty word."

"I don't know what happened either," Kieran responded. "One moment, Dad was representing your father in some venture or other, then he wasn't."

Of course, they'd talked about the bust-up before. But then their only concern was whether the disagreement would endanger their relationship. Now, it had the potential to be much more sinister.

"Were you thinking of my dad when you said there were other possibilities?" asked Ali hesitantly.

"Not really," Kieran replied, still unwilling to expand.

Ali sighed. "It's Rhia, isn't it? You've never trusted her."

Kieran shrugged but did not deny it.

"She always seemed ever so nice to me. You only have a problem with her because she couldn't replace your real mum."

"Maybe," he replied. "But it's more than that." He hesitated before allowing his grievances to spill out. "She's into money in a big way. That's what I can't stand. I reckon she loves it more than she loves Dad. She got pretty rich when she married him, but Dad always stopped her going utterly wild with money. I think she'd do *anything* to get control over his cash. Now there's no one to apply the brakes, she's got everything she wanted. Suddenly, she's even richer, isn't she?"

"Possibly," Ali said. "But isn't it more likely that you are?"

Kieran frowned. "I ... er ... I don't know. I haven't thought about it. I wouldn't want to profit from all this."

"I know." Judging Kieran's need perfectly, Ali suggested, "Let's talk about something else – or just relax."

It seemed callous to engage in small talk under the circumstances so, as the train hurtled south, they were mostly silent.

Jim waved a piece of paper in his commanding officer's direction. "Something for you," he called in triumph.

"Already?" David responded. "What?"

"It's John Evans. He got parole two weeks ago!"

"You're kidding! How come?" He held out his hand for the report. Excitedly, he scanned it. "Oh, yes! This is good. I think you'd better get me a car, Jim."

"Already done, sir."

Cursing the traffic, Jim drove south into the London suburb of Balham. While Evans had been serving fifteen years of his sentence, his solicitors had looked after his assets. The Balham house was not as grand as the one in which the surgeon had killed his wife, but it was more than a home. After so much time in a cell, it was a palace.

David banged on the big door and waited. It was an old and large house, in need of much repair. When the door creaked open, both officers held up their identification. "Detective Inspector Thompson and this is DS Morrow," David announced.

John Evans looked briefly to the heavens and then groaned. "CID. It didn't take you long."

"What do you mean by that, Mr Evans?" David asked smartly.

"Out for two weeks and you're round already. I do know my rights, you know. I know what constitutes police harassment. Once on your records, always a soft target." There was a hint of hysteria in his tone. "You'll try to pin anything on me. My lawyer warned me about you."

"Look," David retorted. "We can come in and ask you a few questions or we can take you back to HQ. Either way, we need some answers. Please yourself. And call your lawyer if you like."

The surgeon was a tall thin man with little hair. His clothing was old-fashioned and looked baggy on him. His hands were large, white and steady. It was easy to imagine them wielding a scalpel. He stood to one side and mumbled, "Better come in."

The living room was spacious but shabby and sparsely decorated. When David dropped into an armchair, a small cloud of dust enveloped him. Jim stood behind his boss and kept his eyes on the suspect. "So," David began, "you join the real world again. Some would say fifteen years isn't long compared to a lifetime."

"I wouldn't," he snapped.

"No, I don't suppose so. Prison couldn't have been easy for a professional man like you."

John Evans eyed the detective with distrust. "If you'd come here for polite conversation you would've brought a bottle. You haven't – so what's it all about?"

"You left court all those years ago, screaming ... what was it?" David consulted Jim's notes. " 'I'll get you, Burrage. You and your family.' "

"Did I?" murmured Evans, as if it were unimportant. "Perhaps, but I don't remember. If I did, it must have been the heat of the moment. The judge, bless him, had just told me I was going to spend the rest of my life behind bars. I'm only human – I might have let off a bit of steam." He scratched his bald head comically then stared directly into David's face and added, "Haven't you heard? Burrage is safe from me. The Assessment Board decided that I'm not a danger to the public. Prison cured me," he stated cynically. "I'm a good boy now! That's why I got parole."

"Yes. I know that." But Evans' dark eyes did not suggest sanity to David. The detective's intuition told him a very different story. He said, "I also heard that you saved the life of a warder in that prison riot last year. That didn't do your case any harm. In fact, I can picture you. Riot all around. Badly injured prison officer. What did you think? Here's a fellow human being who needs my help? Or here's my passport out of prison? Your medical knowledge allowed you to milk the opportunity for parole."

John Evans continued to peer at him defiantly and wildly. "It doesn't matter what you think. It's what the Board thought that counts."

Fifteen years ago, the surgeon's case was notorious. It was rare for a professional man like Evans to be found guilty of common murder. He was convicted because his fingerprints were on the knife, the stab wound was delivered by an expert, and he did not have an alibi – and because the prosecuting barrister was a persuasive performer. Under relentless questioning by Stuart Burrage, Evans broke down in court. He complained about pressure at work, where his mistakes had resulted in the deaths of two patients. He complained about pressure at home. He swore that he loved his wife, but admitted that she nagged him constantly. Because he loved her, he could not retaliate. He took it all, the hen-pecked husband, till he snapped. He wept helplessly in the dock and the prosecution got the result. For the rest of the proceedings, the defendant stared grimly at the floor. Only when he was led away did he look up. As a parting shot, he pointed at Stuart Burrage, threatening him and his family. If anyone in the courtroom was uncertain about the guilty verdict, that final act clinched it. The outburst seemed to prove that he was capable of suddenly flipping and destroying a family – his own or someone else's.

David sprang the important question on him.

"Where were you Saturday afternoon between three and four?"

"Saturday afternoon?" John Evans gazed at the police officers with his head on one side. He was trying to deduce the background to the question. Slowly, a smirk began to appear on his face. "Do you mean someone's had a go at Burrage?" He raised his long arms, about to wave them in triumph and celebration, but decided to curb the impulse.

David merely repeated his question.

"Well, well, well. Sorry to disappoint you, Inspector, but I was ... otherwise engaged."

"Otherwise engaged?" David queried.

There was a short but telling pause before he answered, "I was here, watching the cricket." He nodded towards the television. "Not much else to do these days, thanks to you lot."

"Did you watch it on your own?"

"Yes." He barked his response as if he were issuing a challenge.

"Who was playing?"

Evans grimaced as if he found the question tiresome. "You'll have to do better than that," he mocked. "Middlesex versus Warwickshire. Warwickshire won again."

"As an alibi, it's hardly watertight," David Thompson remarked.

The surgeon shrugged. "It doesn't matter what I say. I know you. You'll pull it apart anyway if you want to – by hook or by crook. A man like Burrage must develop a lot of enemies, not just me, but if you want to blame me for something, I dare say you will. I'm not exactly heartbroken if he's copped it. In fact, nothing would give me greater pleasure."

David rose, declaring, "You'll be hearing from us." With Jim behind him, he made for the front door.

"Well," Evans prompted, "*has* Burrage gone to the great courtroom in the sky?"

Tersely, Detective Inspector Thompson growled, "I think you already know that. I dare say it'll be on local news tonight and all over the papers by morning."

Back in the car, David quizzed his sergeant. "What did you make of our ex-surgeon, ex-con, then?"

Changing into top gear, Jim answered, "Mad as a hatter. Mad as the Parole Board."

"He did plug a hole in a prison warder."

"Only to buy his freedom," Jim rejoined.

"Mmm," David muttered, "I agree. It could be happening all over again. First, Evans' wife, now Stuart Burrage. Both stab wounds were precise. John Evans is an expert surgeon. He didn't have an alibi before and he hasn't got a decent one now. The only thing that's missing so far is his fingerprints on the knife."

"I'll check on that cricket match," Jim offered.

"Don't bother," David replied. "He was right. Middlesex trounced by Warwickshire. All it proves is that he's listened to the news or read this morning's sports pages. There was a *Daily Telegraph* on the table in the corner." He glanced at Jim and said, "You'd better check that Kieran Burrage and the Tankersley girl were really in Scotland on Saturday, though. It's a bit far-fetched but let's not miss anything. They were supposed to be on some sort of swimming club tour."

"OK," Jim responded. "What now?"

"Stuart's junior partner, Daniel Allgrove. I want to ask him about that e-mail message Stuart sent him half an hour before he died. And then I want to know if Allgrove could have got from his place to the Burrages' house within half an hour. After that, Robert Tankersley. See if we can find out what that last report was about. Let's see if we can collar both of them before the news breaks – while there's still an element of surprise."

It was late on Monday afternoon when the detectives were ushered into Daniel Allgrove's cluttered office. The lawyer, trying to look important behind his huge mahogany desk, was dressed to impress in an expensive suit and flamboyant tie. He was used to dealing with police officers. He regarded them with a degree of suspicion and contempt. He saw them as worker ants, crawling everywhere, doing the grubby and unpleasant jobs, to provide fodder for the queens of the legal profession, like himself. "Yes?" he said, waving them towards a couple of chairs. "What can I do for you gents?"

"You can tell me if you got an e-mail message from Stuart Burrage at the weekend."

The lawyer's face screwed up. "Now why would you be interested in that?"

"Did you?"

"Why not ask Stuart? He's working on a case at home today – and waiting for his wife to return from some trip, as I understand it. You could catch up with him at home." Glancing at the detectives' dour expressions, he hesitated and then asked, "Has something happened to him? It has, hasn't it?"

David saw no advantage in denying the crime or prolonging the mystery. He broke the news of Stuart Burrage's death.

Allgrove seemed surprised but not stunned. For a few seconds he was silent, gathering his thoughts, absorbing the implications. He shook his head woefully. Using a respectful whisper, he did his best to express regret at his senior partner's fate, but only succeeded in sounding relieved. "That's ... awful. Poor Stuart – and Rhia."

"Indeed," David replied. "He was murdered perhaps half an hour after he sent you a message, so naturally I'm curious about its contents. Did it arrive here, or at your house?"

"Here, but Stuart knows ... I mean, knew ... that I scan my messages from home with my computer there. So he knew I'd get it anyway. I was just putting the finishing touches to a piece of work when the computer bleeped me to tell me that a message had come in from Stuart. It was just before three."

"How come you know the time so accurately?" David enquired.

Daniel answered, "I was late, hurrying so I could go across to the school field and watch my boy play football. Local league. Three o'clock kick off. Parents have to take an interest, don't you think?"

"Did you go to the match or did the message stop you?"

"I read it quickly. Nothing urgent. He wanted my help with a copyright case. It's a messy and complex business these days, when two companies are at each other's throats over a copyright dispute. It needs careful research so Stuart turned to me. Nothing new in that. He often did when there were complications. I have a talent for it, you know. Anyway, there was something about the Bridge Club in his e-mail as well. A change in venue for the next meeting. That's it. Nothing to keep me from the game."

"Did anyone see you at this football match?"

"What are you suggesting, Inspector Thompson?" Daniel snarled.

"I'm following a line of inquiry – as thoroughly as a lawyer would wish me to."

"Yes, but I don't like your insinuation." He turned away with distaste but answered the question anyway. "Obviously my son saw me supporting on the touch-line. I exchanged words with his trainer late in the game – told him where he was going wrong – so he'd remember I was there as well."

"This message. Can you give a copy?" David asked.

"I don't see why not. But I don't see why I should either."

"It could be important."

"I doubt it," Daniel responded. "It's totally innocuous, I assure you. But, if you're adamant, I suppose I can print you a copy – if you think it'll assist your thorough inquiries." He turned to his computer, clicked the mouse a few times and then mumbled to himself, "Here it is." He clicked once more and then declared, "It'll be with you in a few seconds – for what it's worth." He nodded towards a printer in the corner of the room that had already begun to murmur to itself.

Jim strolled towards it and waited for the emerging piece of paper.

"I'm still ... a bit bewildered, to tell you the truth," Allgrove admitted. "I can't take it in. There'll be changes round here. Life without him is ... hard to imagine." He shook his head again.

Jim handed the print-out to his boss. David's eyes skimmed over it. "Thanks," he said to the lawyer.

"No problem," he replied. "Is there anything else I can do? I must go and see Rhia. Give her my commiserations."

"You can provide me with a list of people who might have reason to want Stuart out of the way. You know, disgruntled clients, violent crooks he put away. Jim here will help as well."

Allgrove shrugged. "OK. I'll put my mind to it – when I have time – and let you know." He exhaled loudly and added, "Now, if you gentlemen have got all you need, and I'm sure you have, I'd like to get on. As you'll appreciate, I have a busy time ahead of me. Important cases that will now be my responsibility. Clients to reassure."

David and Jim left. In the car, Jim declared, "Slimy, wasn't he? And arrogant."

"He's a young ambitious lawyer," David said with a wry smile. "It's part of the deal."

"He wasn't exactly devastated," Jim observed.

"No. Better contact his son's football team. Check out what he said. Right now, though," the inspector said, looking carefully at his watch, "I want you to drive to the Burrages' house. We don't need to go in. I just want to know how long it takes. Keep to the speed limit."

The journey took fourteen minutes. David

muttered, "He could have left his house at three and made it here in plenty of time to commit murder. He'd be back by three forty-five. In time for the second half. He said he'd spoken to the coach *late* in the game. Interesting."

"The e-mail seems innocent enough, though," Jim put in. "Nothing to incite murder."

David read it again. "I agree. I doubt if we'd have got it quite so easily if there was something incriminating in it. Still, as junior partner, he already had enough motive." Tapping the paper, he added, "I'll take a look at this Bridge Club and the copyright case anyway. No stone unturned to get to the bottom of this one."

By the time that the detectives reached Robert Tankersley's house, all of the family had been reunited. Robert had come in from work and Ali had returned from Edinburgh with news of Kieran's father. DI Thompson had lost the element of surprise.

"I'm ... shocked," Robert stated as he paced the large lounge. "It's a disaster. We did business, me and Stuart. Not recently, but in the past. And, of course, Ali's going out with his son. I hope Kieran takes it OK."

"What sort of business, Mr Tankersley?"

"I sell electronic equipment. Stuart gave me legal advice."

"What sort of electronic equipment needs legal advice?"

Robert Tankersley stopped walking and peered at the detective. "Our equipment's used in all sorts of devices, but it includes missile guidance systems. There are strict – and complicated – controls on who you can sell arms to. Stuart kept my company on the right side of the law."

"But you hadn't sought his advice recently?"

"No. Once he'd put me on the straight and narrow, there wasn't any need. If the regulations on arms controls had changed, I would've been banging on his door again."

Behind David, Jim watched Mrs Tankersley and Ali. Mrs Tankersley sat stiffly, clearly nervous, but nodding almost continuously as if to support her husband. Ali frowned at her dad's last answer. She did not believe that he had told the truth.

"Can you explain," David pronounced, "why Stuart Burrage's last action was to begin a report that concerned you?"

"Me? Strange. No, I don't know anything about that, I'm afraid. What did it say?"

"Next to nothing. He didn't get the opportunity."

"I see," Ali's father replied, head bowed.

"Mr Tankersley. I'd like to speak to you in private for a moment," David said.

"I don't have anything to hide," he snapped.

"Maybe you don't. Maybe I do."

Robert shrugged, led the detective into a small study, and closed the door impatiently. "What is it?" he muttered, plainly annoyed.

David noted that, in the corner of the room, there was a desk and a state-of-the-art personal computer. Robert Tankersley also worked in electronics. Obviously he *was* familiar with computers. "What were you doing on Saturday afternoon?" asked the detective.

"What? Am I a suspect?"

"I am just trying to assemble a picture of what everyone was doing when he died. That's all," the police officer replied coolly.

"I assure you, Inspector Thompson, I had nothing to do with it."

"So where were you?"

"Shopping," he answered. "With my wife."

"Thank you," the detective replied. "Wait in here a moment, please."

David went back into the living room and asked Mrs Tankersley what she was doing on Saturday afternoon.

"What I always do," she answered timidly. "I go shopping in town."

"On your own?"

"No," she replied. "With Robert."

Fleetingly, Ali frowned again.

As the police officers left, David Thompson asked Ali, "Did you leave Kieran with Rhia?"

"Yes," she muttered. "They probably need time on their own – to sort themselves out. It won't be easy for either of them."

David nodded in sombre agreement. "True."

The taxi had pulled into Kieran's drive, dropped him off, and then whisked Ali away, back to her own house. Kieran had stood for a moment in the porch and breathed deeply before unlocking the door and going in.

The reunion with his stepmother was an awkward, unnatural event. She rushed to him and clasped him as if, suddenly and inexplicably, the death of his father had drawn them closer together. Kieran did not believe that it had. Reconciliation was not that easy. He did not reap any comfort from her embrace and he withdrew from her arms as soon as he could.

There were tears in Rhia's eyes and she sobbed, "Thanks for coming back. I ... I'm sorry. Sorry about your dad."

"Yes," Kieran mumbled. He could not cry. He had run out of tears when his mum died and later when she was replaced by Rhia. It didn't mean that he couldn't mourn his father but, for Kieran, it would be done with dry eyes and in private.

"I can see you're upset," Rhia whimpered.

"Yes," Kieran repeated. Utter turmoil would have been a more apt description. He felt that he ought to be even more anguished at the loss of his father. He thought that he might just have hugged the person who had murdered him. If so, she was putting on a convincing show of grief. He didn't want to be alone in the house with only Rhia – a stranger really – from now on. He didn't want to share his life with a stepmother that he resented. He wanted it to be like it was all those years ago – before his mum died and before his dad became famous and unapproachable.

"Where is he?" he asked quietly.

"Your dad? You mean, where have they taken ... his body?"

"Yes."

"The police took him away. There can't be a funeral until after the investigation." Fresh tears appeared again. "It's horrible." Her words came out almost as if she were underwater. Her eyes were red, set in a pallid complexion. She blew her nose and then muttered, "If you want to see him ... I'm sure David Thompson would arrange it."

Kieran didn't know what he wanted. And he didn't know what was expected of him. Seven years ago, he was with his mother in hospital when she died. Then, there were no choices to be made. He had not gained the experience needed to deal with his father's death. "I'm not sure," he said. "I'll think about it, I guess." He'd known enough about the manner of his mother's death to despise it. Now, he realized that he knew hardly anything about his dad's murder. "Where did it happen?" he muttered.

In reply, Rhia looked fearfully through the hall towards the door to the study. "While he was working at the computer."

The door was almost always open. Now, it was shut as if it could protect them from what had happened beyond. The study was sealed like a tomb.

"How did he...?"

Rhia sighed. "Didn't they tell you? They think someone came in through the back door, picked up a kitchen knife and..." Her hand shot to her throat as if she could feel the blade herself. She slumped into a seat. "Why didn't he come to France with me? Damn it!"

Kieran knew that he should go to her side and comfort her. But he didn't know how and he didn't feel inclined.

Rhia shook her head slowly. "I don't know what we'll do without him."

For a moment, Kieran was touched by her torment. "No," he said, almost tenderly, "but we'll sort something out, I guess." Then, still nonplussed by the situation, he added rather feebly, "I'll go and brew up some tea." He knew that tea was not a magical remedy for anything but at least, in making it, he would be doing something useful – and Rhia would interpret his action as kindness. Under the circumstances, it was the most sympathy that he could show her.

In the middle of the night, Kieran got out of bed and padded furtively to the study. He felt attracted towards it, like iron to a magnet. He didn't understand why but he wanted to be where his dad had drawn his last breath. It would be Kieran's personal commemoration for his father. He turned the handle of the study door slowly and quietly, as if he were the intruder. Silently, he opened the door and entered. The room felt colder than the rest of the house. It was nothing supernatural, Kieran knew. It was just that he felt chilled inside. He tiptoed, like his dad's assailant must have done, towards the desk. He touched the back of the chair but let go immediately. It felt like ice. He shivered. He could almost feel the presence of his father, working away, oblivious to everything around him. Once, it would have been Kieran, holding out a game or a school report, who would have remained unnoticed. On Saturday, it was a murderer with a knife. Kieran's spine tingled. His dad did not deserve to die alone at the whim of some thug.

He turned and hurried away. The dismal study evoked the stale atmosphere of sudden and violent death. He could take it no longer.

3

The next day, a message arrived on David Thompson's desk. The Strathclyde Police had confirmed that Kieran Burrage and Ali Tankersley had taken part in a swimming gala in Glasgow on Friday evening. Kieran had come second in the individual medley and Ali had won the 200 metres backstroke. They were also seen at the team's party on Saturday night. It was not impossible for one or both of them to have returned to London between the two events but it was unlikely. They were probably both in the clear. Detective Inspector Thompson also received the pathologist's preliminary conclusions. After reading the findings, he felt that he had to return to Rhia Burrage and ask her another question. He was not looking forward to it.

In the Burrages' living room, feeling decidedly uncomfortable, the police officer coughed and then declared, "I'm sorry, Rhia, but I have to explore every avenue." To get it over with, he plunged straight in. "I have to ask you your whereabouts in Paris on Saturday afternoon."

Rhia was much more composed today but her innate poise, diminished by her husband's death, showed no sign of returning. As she listened to David's question, her neglected face expressed patience more than anger. She was disappointed that his duty outweighed their friendship but she realized that it would. The man trusted her, no doubt, but the detective in him could not afford to be swayed by familiarity. She expected David to become Detective Inspector Thompson and to investigate her movements. She was prepared for the questioning.

"I know you have to do your job." She sighed. "It means you've found out when he died, I suppose."

"Yes," the detective answered. "I've just had the report from pathology. It's consistent with the information from his computer. Both suggest three-thirty on Saturday afternoon."

Rhia nodded sadly. "Saturday. Let me think." She stared for a moment at the ceiling and then continued, "My art day. Pompidou Centre in the morning, the Louvre in the afternoon."

"And ... er ... I don't suppose Customs stamped

your passport? In France, they don't really bother these days."

Before Rhia could answer, Kieran came into the room to see who had arrived. He looked pale and unkempt – as if he hadn't slept all night.

Distracted, the detective turned to him and murmured, "I'm sorry about your father, Kieran. And I'm sorry we had to drag you back early. We all thought it for the best, though."

"Yes, it's OK," he replied dully. "Am I interrupting something?"

"David's just asking me a few questions," Rhia admitted. "Mainly about where I was on Saturday afternoon. Three-thirty. That's when ... you know. Your dad's computer recorded the time, apparently."

"I see," Kieran mumbled. "Do you want me to make myself scarce?"

"No," his stepmother replied. "Not as far as I'm concerned anyway." She looked at David in case he objected to an audience. He signified his indifference with a shrug so Rhia continued, "Where were we? Passport. No. They looked at it, but that's all. If you need confirmation that I wasn't here, though, you can check with British Midland. I flew with them from Heathrow to Charles de Gaulle airport. They'll have records, I suppose."

"Yes, I'll have to do that."

Kieran did not interrupt. He leaned against the wall and listened. It was hardly a grilling. The detective appeared to be satisfied with Rhia's response. He did not seem to be considering that she could have sneaked back into the country on Saturday morning and slipped back to Paris in the evening. She could have made the extra journey easily, using a ferry or the tunnel. His closeness with her was blinding him to the possibility. Almost immediately Kieran lost confidence in David Thompson. Kieran did not know about French Customs policy, but he thought that a thorough police officer would have asked to see her passport just in case it had been stamped on Saturday.

"How's it going, in general?" Rhia asked.

David relaxed a little. "Well... Still checking. We've got a number of leads. We're looking at alibis and motives. There's one particularly strong suspect, just out of jail. Stuart prosecuted him for murder some fifteen years ago. Name of John Evans. And there's some other possibilities. Basically, no one's out of the reckoning yet – except you two, of course," he added quickly. "You were both miles away. Besides, I don't think for one minute..."

Rhia smiled limply. "You don't have to mother me, David. I won't be off your hit list till you've checked out my trip to Paris."

"That's just a formality, I'm sure." He was almost blushing. He pointed to a framed photograph of Stuart and Rhia and asked, "Do you have a copy of that – or something similar showing the two of you?"

"Yes. I'll get one for you." Getting to her feet like a doddery old woman and fiddling inside a cupboard, she enquired, "Do you need it for a picture of Stuart or me?"

"Well, for both really."

Giving him a photograph from an album, she commented, "That's your polite way of saying for me."

He did not deny it. Instead, he said, "There's a couple more things. Can you give me the names and addresses of the regulars at your Bridge Club?"

"The Bridge Club?" Rhia was amazed.

"Yes." The police officer explained, "One of his last communications was about the club so I need to check out the members."

Rhia shrugged. "OK. I can make you a list now, if you want." She went for a pen and paper.

"Thanks," David replied.

Once she had jotted down the details and given him the list, she added, "You said there were a couple of things."

"Oh, yes," he replied. "Did someone leave a fingerprint kit with you?"

"Yes," answered Rhia. "He put it in the fridge."

"Good." Addressing Kieran, the detective said, "Sorry about this but I need your prints – to eliminate them from any others we've found. OK?

If you come into the kitchen, I'll help you through it right now. Then I can take them away with me. Get it over with."

Kieran shrugged and followed the officer.

Back at headquarters, David turned to Jim and said, "Well, we have to go through the motions. The Louvre must be riddled with video cameras. They'll have captured Rhia on tape. Get on to it, will you? I'll authorize a trip to Paris for you. Check the airports as well. Heathrow and Charles de Gaulle security cameras. You should look into her British Midland booking, I guess, but it won't mean much – not now Paris is just round the corner by train. Theoretically, she could have come back into the country on Saturday. It's more important to sort out the security pictures so we can eliminate her once and for all."

"There's something not quite right about all this," Ali commented.

Kieran put his hands on the side of the swimming pool, heaved and twisted. Dripping water that had been warmed by the sun, he sat next to Ali. His body was perfect. Training had given him broad shoulders, upper body strength and flexibility. His trunk tapered to a lean waist and his legs were slender but muscle-packed. Ali was shorter but built to the same design. Supple yet powerful. If they had been the same height and walking side by side, their ample shoulders would have kept them apart. Now, both of them were clad in swimming suits and dangled their legs in the pool. Kieran wiped the water from his face and enquired, "What do you mean?"

"I'm not sure," Ali responded. "But something strange is going on. Last night, after the policemen left my place, Dad disappeared straight away. He made a bolt for the study and occupied the phone for an age."

"So, he was telling all his business contacts about ... Dad," Kieran suggested.

"Possibly. But ... Oh, I don't know. Earlier, Mum and Dad lied to the police – twice maybe. I'm sure. Mum said she went shopping with Dad on Saturday. Well, Dad hates shopping. He always leaves it to Mum. And he didn't say that he'd fallen out with your dad, just that he didn't need his advice any more. And he implied there was no big bust-up by saying he would've consulted your dad in the future if need be. I don't believe that."

"Maybe not," Kieran replied. "But it strikes me he was just taking precautions. He didn't want to admit he's got a motive of some sort so he left out the argument. And he didn't want to admit to an opportunity so your parents agreed on an alibi. They must have worked it out after you told them about Dad but before the police arrived." Kieran swept his hand through his wet hair. "Perhaps they were lying but you can't really blame them – not unless ... but I can't believe that."

"I'm not so sure now," Ali said in a quaking voice. Her father's lies had persuaded her that he *was* a suspect. "Something funny's going on, I tell you, and it's about my dad, your dad, and business."

Kieran grunted. "Business," he murmured derisively.

Both Ali and Kieran were disillusioned with their fathers' trades. Kieran believed that lawyers were committed more to their clients than to the truth. Ali despaired that her dad's computer chips, so ingenious and so creative, were used to kill people. It was cruel and perverse. To Kieran and Ali it seemed that both of their fathers were prepared to sacrifice conscience for cash.

The same substitute of cash for conscience lay behind the pool. When Kieran began to develop a considerable talent for swimming, his dad had the pool built in the garden. It was a busy father's way of encouraging Kieran. Spending a few thousand pounds was much easier than giving up precious time to take a real interest in Kieran's progress.

"I've just had a terrible thought," Ali said, staring in horror at her boyfriend and shuddering as if the water had suddenly turned cold. "You don't think *you're* in danger, do you?"

Kieran shrugged. "I've been wondering that myself. It depends if Dad was the only target, I suppose." He put his hand on Ali's shoulder. "It depends what you believe about the motive. If someone's got something against the Burrages, yes, I might be. Especially if it's something against both Dad and me. But I can't be absolutely sure what we're dealing with. I suppose it *could* be someone with a grudge against Dad's firm. Maybe Daniel Allgrove is the one in danger. Maybe everyone is – it could have been a random choice by a serial killer."

"But if it *is* a family vendetta... Well, whoever did it, he could be watching us right now. It's scary."

Kieran tried to smile. He shuffled closer to her and put his arm round her shoulders. "I shouldn't think so," he replied in a reassuring voice. He kissed her forehead. As he did it, a movement in the window of Rhia's room caught his eye. He withdrew and whispered sullenly, "But I wouldn't be so sure it was a he."

"You're thinking of Rhia again," Ali deduced.

"Yes."

Glancing round to check that they were alone in the garden, Ali argued in a hushed voice, "But she seems desperately unhappy to me."

"I know," Kieran mumbled. Rhia had always been so immaculate, more like a perfectly pro-grammed robot than flesh and blood, that it was hard to imagine her in distress. He had never seen her sick or scruffy or dishevelled. He had hardly

53

ever seen her without the embellishments of make-up and jewellery. Now, she looked so drab that it came as a revelation to him that she could apparently suffer like a normal human being. "She's a social animal but she hasn't left the house. She just mopes around. She's either shocked and hurt – or good at pretending."

In Rhia's defence, Ali murmured, "I think you're too hard on her."

"Like you're too hard on your dad, thinking of him as a suspect?"

Ali managed a grin. "Yes. I suppose so. But, don't forget, Rhia was in Paris at the time."

"Yes, well, the police are checking that, so we'll know soon – if they do it properly."

Ali peered into his face and said softly, "You've been shaken by all this. You asked me out here because you thought you could swim it out of your system. You're more shaken than you'll admit to."

"Perhaps. It's just that..." He sighed. He had always been open and honest with Ali and, as far as he knew, she had always been the same with him. This was not the time to change. He needed her now more than ever before. "I know Dad didn't bother with me much over the last few years but, even so, I feel lonely without him, Ali. Like I'm a stranger round here. When Rhia moved in, she turned the house into *her* place. At least when Dad came home, he reminded me of how it was – the good times. Now he's gone, I'm a stranger in her home. It's as if there's no one to … to love me, I suppose."

Ali turned and hugged him. "Oh, Kieran! I'm sorry. But you've got me, you know."

"Yes. I don't want to lose you as well."

"Don't worry," she said into his ear. "You won't."

Kieran could not sleep on Tuesday night either. After hours of shifting position under a single sheet and peeping at the clock, he sat up and listened. The house was quiet. Rhia must be sleeping. Again, he was lured to the study. This time, it had more to do with Rhia than with his father. Even so, when he went in, trying not to make a sound, he felt apprehensive. It was illogical because the evil had long since gone, yet he could not help himself. In his mind, the room would always be blighted and spooky. He faltered for a few seconds but told himself that he was being silly. Regaining his resolve, he headed for the cabinet where his dad had kept all of the important documents. Slowly, he pulled the drawer open. It made a noise that was probably not loud but, in the silence of the night, sounded like thunder.

Kieran hesitated, waiting in case there were any tell-tale footsteps from upstairs. After a minute, everything remained still. He sighed with relief. Before he resumed, he crept back to the door and closed it. He could not risk being discovered by Rhia. Besides, he would have to put on a lamp at some point. Closing the door would contain the light but it also reminded Kieran of being sealed in a crypt. Trying to ignore his discomfort, he returned to the cabinet and opened it further. He fiddled amongst the insurance policies, cheque books, birth certificates and other documents until he found what he wanted. He clutched three passports but, in the gloom, he could not distinguish one from another. Instead, he grabbed all three and took them to the computer desk.

Praying that the light would not give him away, he clicked on the desk lamp. Blinking in the sudden glare, Kieran selected Rhia's passport and flicked through its pages. Last year, she'd taken a holiday in Antigua. Kieran found the entry marked, "Antigua and Barbuda," but beyond it the rest of the pages were blank. Kieran was not sure whether to be disappointed or relieved. He was none the wiser. Rhia was right that the French Customs officers had not stamped the book at all. On Saturday, she might have returned home. Equally, she might never have been to Paris.

As he turned off the lamp and gathered up the passports, he contemplated the possibility that she had never left in the first place. He could not believe that Rhia would swear that she'd been to Paris if she hadn't. She'd know that it would be simple for the police to check on international travel. Surely, she would never get away with such a blatant lie. Shaking his head, he put the passports back into their place. As he did so, it struck him that a copy of his dad's will was likely to be somewhere in the drawer. Yet he decided not to search for it. It could take a while to find and even longer to understand. Besides, he considered it as private. While he remained suspicious of Rhia, he believed that it was legitimate to meddle with her things in the pursuit of the truth but he drew the line at prying into his father's will. It would be like grave-robbing. He closed the drawer, praying that it would not screech, and then slunk back up the stairs.

He gasped aloud and nearly fell backwards when the landing light suddenly blazed.

Above him, Rhia appeared like a ghost hovering between one world and the next. Wearing an expensive silk dressing-gown, she was bleary-eyed and haggard. In a slurred voice, she asked, "Can't you sleep either?"

"Er ... no."

"The doctor gave me some pills to help, but they don't seem to do the trick all through the night." She yawned.

"Sorry if I disturbed you," Kieran stammered. "It's a muggy night. Just went down for a bit of fresh air."

"Did you go into the study?"

"No ... I mean ... yes." Kieran admitted it in case she had heard him coming out of the study.

More awake, Rhia murmured, "Nothing to be ashamed about. I go in sometimes. It's curious. Sort of haunted. Creepy, but at least I feel close to him there." She looked down at her stepson, still clinging to the banister. "I loved your father, you know, Kieran. And, while he didn't have the time to be much of a family man, I think you loved him too. We have that in common." She paused and added, "As well as an inability to sleep. So let's not fight each other. Agreed? We're on the same side."

Kieran could not bring himself to make peace but he was not sure enough of her guilt to make war. "Are we?" he muttered dubiously.

"Yes," she insisted. Not waiting for him to reply, she said, "Now, I'm just going to the bathroom, then back to bed. Are you going to try and settle?"

He began to trudge up the remaining steps. "I suppose so."

"Good night, then," she mumbled as she glided along the passage like a lost and tortured soul.

4

Detective Inspector Thompson drew a blank on the Bridge Club. If any member had harboured a dislike for Stuart Burrage, it was well concealed. The detective had failed to ascertain a single strong motive among the members. The only ill-feeling towards the Burrages resulted from the fact that they won all of the time. As David would have anticipated, Stuart was a class player. But no one kills an opponent for winning a game of cards.

In examining the contents of Stuart Burrage's computer, Kate had left no byte unturned. Even so, she had failed to cast any more light on his murder. The forensic report was disappointing as well. The scene of the crime was clean. All of the fibres identified so far belonged to Stuart, Rhia or Kieran.

Only the Burrages' fingerprints were on the door handles. The keyboard, mouse, desk and chair were covered in Stuart's prints. As expected, the knife bore Rhia's fingerprints, but there were no others. The killer had been very careful. He could not have wiped away his own prints because the cleaning would have smeared Rhia's. He must have worn gloves.

Jim returned from France bearing a large box full of videotapes. "The good news is, I got all we need. Both airports and the Louvre co-operated. That's a lot of cameras. So the bad news is, there's several days of viewing here."

David grimaced. He had not joined the police force and risen to his current rank to watch a television screen all day. He delegated to his team. "OK," he replied. "Assemble as many people as you want – and the same number of TVs – so you can get through it pretty quickly. I'll get copies of a photograph of Rhia so you can tape one to each telly. Then get their heads down for the search."

Jim groaned and muttered, "It's excitement all the way in the police force."

"Remember the time difference, as well. They're an hour ahead of us over there." Leaving his sergeant to get on with the tedious sifting job, David went to consult Daniel Allgrove again.

Stuart's junior partner, suddenly in the hot seat of the business, seemed to be stressed. It couldn't have been easy for him to take on the responsibility of being in charge and, at the same time, to cope with two people's jobs. Consequently, he had not had much time to assemble a list of Stuart's enemies. "Before my time," Daniel said, "there was a surgeon who was supposed to have threatened him in court. Let me think. What was his name?"

David interjected, "John Evans. We're working on that lead already. Any more?"

Daniel Allgrove sucked in air audibly. "Several, but I doubt that many would be capable of murder."

"Which might?" the detective inquired.

"A couple of years ago, he helped a police officer out of a tricky situation when a suspect died mysteriously in his custody. The victim had a brother. Surname of Pascoe. Rumour had it that he was as bent as his brother. He'd bear Stuart a grudge, no doubt. But, personally, I would have thought the police officer himself was a more obvious target." Daniel stared momentarily at the ceiling and then continued, "He prosecuted a terrorist accused of murder. He was released after a few years because the forensic evidence was found to be flawed. I wouldn't dream of telling you your job but, even if terrorism isn't big business here any more, you might want to think about a revenge attack. I'm too busy to find the details but my secretary can supply them. There are a few other possibilities but, to be honest, I don't give them much credence. And I'm pretty astute in these matters. I think you're wasting your time."

"Perhaps," David conceded, "but I still want to check everything – even the remote possibilities – so I'd like your secretary's information."

"As you wish," the lawyer responded tersely.

"I also wanted to ask you about the copyright case mentioned in Stuart's message."

Daniel expressed surprise. "I hardly think there would be grounds for murder there," he replied. "We're talking respectable businessmen here."

"Tell me about it," David prompted.

"You're supposed to be an intelligent man so you'll appreciate the ... sensitivity. I have to preserve my client's confidentiality. But…"

Patiently, trying not to take offence, David reminded him, "It *is* for Stuart."

"Yes, I know," Daniel replied. "I can tell you this. We're ... I'm acting for Xenon Computing. The company's got good reason to believe that a copyright on one of its products has been breached by Megaware. When we show our proof, it's more than likely that Megaware will settle out of court. Xenon stands to pick up ten million. Now it's in my hands, I might secure an even better settlement. Big business."

"I haven't heard of either company. Are they well known?"

"No. They're both small outfits, employing a few

computer whizz kids. But they supply some of the big players. Megaware's not independent, though. It's owned by CompuTech."

"And who's behind CompuTech?"

"No idea," Daniel admitted. "Stuart would have found out, I should think, but I didn't get a report from him and I've had no time to chase it up."

"Mmm." DI Thompson did not elucidate further. He rose and thanked Daniel for his time. "It's been interesting," he remarked. "I may need to speak to you again. I'll be in touch."

On Wednesday, determined to escape for a while from Rhia's homemade morgue, Kieran went with Ali to the coffee bar in the sports centre. There, half the swimming team and half of their school seemed to be a permanent fixture. Everyone knew each other. When Kieran walked in, the cordial buzz suddenly ceased. He could have been a conspicuous stranger strolling deliberately into the saloon in a corny western. The boy with no name. The boy with no father. He wanted to shout at them, "It's only me. Kieran. I haven't changed. No need for the hush." Of course, he didn't shout anything. He just smiled limply at all of the apprehensive faces that turned towards him. He didn't want sympathy or special treatment. He was trying to evade the regular reminders of his father's fate. He just wanted normal company. But his friends did not know how to react. They had all read about the murder in the papers. Commenting on it could upset Kieran. Ignoring it would be heartless. The uncomfortable pause continued until Ali broke the spell by nudging him and muttering, "Come on. Let's get a drink."

Seizing the opportunity to be the centre of attention, Mike Spruzen strode up to Kieran and asked, "How are you?"

Out of habit, Kieran merely grunted in reply.

Without listening, Mike responded, "That's good." He was an incomparable backstroker and an incorrigible pest. He never said hello to anyone. Instead, he always greeted people by asking, "How are you?" He wasn't interested in the reply, though. Responses of "Great, thanks," and, "Appalling," met with the same indifferent and distracted murmur, "Good, good." All of his acquaintances had long since learned that a proper response to his casual question was not worthy of the effort. Mike was concerned only for himself. He also seemed to believe that he looked cool and tough if he drank a few beers. He loved to recount his vast store of drunken adventures, over and over again, to impress anyone who would listen. With each telling a new, fantastic twist was added and the girl in his arms grew more and more stunning. Alcohol seemed to stimulate his imagination and his powers of exaggeration.

Rescuing Kieran again, Ali asked Mike, "How's your shoulder?"

Mike rubbed the injury that had kept him out of the Scottish trip. "Still sore," he said. "Did I tell you how I did it?"

"Yes," Kieran muttered.

Sitting down at their table, he began, "It was funny, looking back, but I wish I hadn't missed Scotland. I had to drink on my own." He giggled at a thought that would not stay private for too long. "It was drinking that got me injured in the first place. Wicked."

"We know," Ali and Kieran said in chorus.

"But did I tell you what happened after I fell down the bank?" Without waiting for a reply, he cracked on enthusiastically. "Well, I landed right by the track. I could've reached out and touched the rail if my shoulder hadn't hurt so much. Good job I didn't, though, because this Intercity flew past. Almost hit me, it did. That would have been curtains. You'd have had to scrape me off at Euston. And you should've heard this gorgeous girl I was with. Thought it had taken my arm off, she did. Scream? She was almost louder than the train! Anyway," he concluded, "I really came over to talk about you guys, not me. Sorry to hear about your old man, Kieran. Have the police got whoever did it?"

Kieran sighed. He did not expect a great deal of

diplomacy from Mike but his flippant enquiry was hard to take. "No," he breathed. "They're investigating."

"Good job you two were in Scotland. Great alibi."

Kieran's mouth fell open but Mike's comment was so tactless that he could not reply.

Ali was less inhibited. "You oaf! Why don't you think before you speak? No one would accuse Kieran of ... hurting his own father. And if we'd been here maybe it wouldn't have... Anyway, just shut up, Mike!"

Normally, Ali let her life follow the line of least resistance. She wasn't lazy, just relaxed about life. That's what Kieran liked about her. When a whirlwind raged all around, she was the tranquil centre. But, when she felt someone had been wronged, she could let fly. Seconds later, she would be relaxed again as if she had rid herself of all her anger in one effective outburst.

"Just asking," Mike mumbled as he retreated.

Ali put her hand on Kieran's leg and whispered, "Still pleased you came, then?" She smiled mischievously at him.

"Well," Kieran replied, "I didn't know Mike would be here, did I?"

Some of the others made up for it. A few friends dared to approach their table and murmur in embarrassed voices, "Sorry about your father, Kieran. It's ... awful. If there's anything I can do..."

Kieran smiled and murmured, "Thanks. It's OK. I'm just trying to carry on. Moping around doesn't solve anything."

Each visitor would nod and reply, "Good for you."

After a while, he was pleased that he'd decided to return to normal life – if only for a few minutes.

Jim's team worked well into the night. It was easy to concentrate on the comings and goings on screen for the first fifteen minutes. It was even amusing. Some people's outlandish dress sense was fascinating. Suitcases that burst open in the airport lounge provided occasional distraction. Spotting the pickpockets became a spectator sport. But, after a while, the entertainment wore thin. It was like watching a tedious ice-skating competition in the hope of seeing a dramatic fall. The endless surveillance tapes numbed the eyes and brain.

It was worth the effort, though. The cameras had witnessed Rhia's departure from Heathrow, arrival at Charles de Gaulle airport, her return journey, and her visit to the Louvre at the exact time that her husband had been killed.

In the early hours, after he'd dismissed the rest of his team, Jim edited the various extracts on to one convenient tape, ready for DI Thompson in the morning.

5

"**Y**ou look a bit rough."

"I know. I'm not sleeping much."

Ali looked at her troubled boyfriend with sympathy. "Is that because of your dad – or because of Rhia?"

"I don't know. A bit of both, I expect."

Ali shook her head. "You really believe that Rhia ... killed your dad, don't you? Despite the fact that she's obviously cut up about it – and she wasn't even in the country at the time."

"It sounds crazy but, yes, I do," Kieran admitted. He was convinced that Rhia's greed was sufficient to provide a motive for murder. "If she was out of the country, I just don't know how she did it, that's all."

"Neither do I," retorted Ali. She was surprised that Kieran clung to his hunch even when it was apparent that Rhia could not be the killer. "You're letting a grudge get in the way of your judgement," she suggested. "There's no evidence against her. Rhia's OK. And she couldn't have done it – even if you'd like to prove she did to get her back for taking your mum's place."

Kieran scowled. "It's not just that."

"What else is it, then?"

"Lots of little things, I guess," answered Kieran.

"Like what?"

"Well, like when she wanted to buy this really flashy Mercedes. Dad said we didn't need it, stopped her, and she went into an almighty grump. Same thing when she decided we should have a holiday villa in Antigua. Dad said we wouldn't use it enough to make it worthwhile. She hit the roof."

"That's supposed to convince me she'd kill for cash?" Ali responded. "Sure it's gross, but it sounds pretty flimsy to me."

"It's not the only thing. You know, the more I think about it, the more I realize I don't know anything about her. I don't even know what she did before she met Dad. She never talks about her past. Perhaps she's hiding something. And about this time last year, just after her father died, I think, she used to go off a lot. No idea what she was up to. She didn't talk about that either."

"Look," Ali said. "Why don't you ask to see that policeman when he gets proof that she was in Paris? David Thompson. I bet he'd talk to you about it. Maybe he'll be able to convince you that she didn't do it."

"No," Kieran replied. "I couldn't. Besides, he's Rhia's friend. I'm not convinced he'll do a proper job anyway. He *wants* to clear her name. Hardly unbiased."

"Maybe. But just because he's biased, it doesn't make her guilty."

In the event, Kieran didn't have a choice. His presence was requested at the police station. Detective Inspector Thompson apologized for inconveniencing him and explained that he'd received some videotapes from the airports and the Louvre in Paris. He was satisfied that the security tapes showed Rhia leaving the country on Thursday 21st July, returning on Monday 25th July, and strolling round the art gallery from two fifteen to four thirty on the Saturday in between. For the investigation, though, he wanted confirmation by someone close to her.

David positioned Kieran in front of a television and turned on the video. "We've got hours of tapes, but you're just getting the edited highlights," he quipped, clearly in a good mood. "The first few sequences are from Heathrow last Thursday. See?" He pointed to the screen where a woman in a white coat and carrying a single suitcase crossed the airport entrance. It could have been almost anyone but the woman did look like Rhia. Then the angle changed. The woman, definitely Rhia, approached the check-in desk. "Well?" David prompted. "This is the British Midland desk. Would you say that's your stepmother?"

Kieran nodded. "Yes, it is." Rhia walked out of camera shot but not yet out of Kieran's reckoning.

The next pictures showed Rhia arriving in Paris. The bottom right-hand corner of the screen showed the date and time. David Thompson reminded him that France was an hour ahead of British time. "Here we are," the police officer announced. "This is the important bit. The Louvre. Saturday. Three-thirty our time. Four-thirty over there."

There was no doubt whatsoever. Now draped in a pale green dress and a loose jacket, Rhia ambled into shot and then stood still in front of a huge canvas. She could have been posing but really she was just lost in admiration for the painting. Kieran nodded again and had to admit it. "Yes, that's Rhia all right."

Mechanically, he watched the clips of Rhia's return to England, again wearing the white coat, and declared a positive identification whenever David Thompson requested it.

When the final picture faded, the detective said, "Mmm. There we have it." He seemed relieved.

"Don't get me wrong, Kieran," he added. "I never believed that Rhia ... was involved, but I had to prove it." Plainly, he had no wish to point the finger at a friend and, by eliminating her from his inquiries, he was one small step nearer the culprit.

In contrast, Kieran was almost disappointed, but he hid it from the police. Unlike David Thompson, he had always suspected Rhia.

"That's all I need," David said, putting his hand briefly on Kieran's shoulder. "Thanks for coming in. I know all this isn't easy for you."

Kieran stood up. "It's OK," he mumbled. It seemed that he wasn't the only one with a great alibi, to quote Mike. Rhia's was cast-iron. Before he left, he asked, "Did you get any fingerprints or anything like that?"

The detective shook his head. "I'm afraid not. The only fingerprints were yours, your dad's and Rhia's. Our man must have been gloved."

While a junior member of the team escorted Kieran out of the police station, David and Jim compared notes with two sergeants who had been given the brief of researching Megaware and CompuTech. They had delved into both companies and discovered something relevant. "Megaware's a subsidiary of CompuTech," they reported, "and CompuTech's owned – at arm's length – by Alpha Systems."

"And Alpha Systems?" David checked, expecting another twist.

The officers grinned at him, plainly pleased with themselves. "Alpha Systems has a managing director with the name of Robert Tankersley. Thought you might be interested, Guv."

"Tankersley?" he exclaimed. "You're not kidding I'm interested." He absorbed the information for a few moments and then thought aloud. "Stuart Burrage used to advise Tankersley. Now he doesn't. Stuart wouldn't have known Tankersley was hiding behind Megaware when he took on Xenon's case. Since then he must have found out that, at the end of the day, he was fighting Tankersley! Then it'd be a case of loyalty to a friend versus the case. Knowing Stuart, he'd stick with the case. He didn't like to drop anything. Like a dog with a bone. For him, letting go would smack of failure. He'd also confront the problem, you know. He was like that. Bet he went to Tankersley and admitted he was acting for a business that had got Megaware in its sights. They'd have fallen out, no doubt. Stuart would disassociate himself from Tankersley rather than lose the case to protect him."

Jim carried on the logic. "It makes sense. If Tankersley's daughter knew they'd had a bust-up, she wouldn't believe her dad when he said to us he would have done business with Burrage again. And she didn't, I'm sure. She didn't believe his alibi either, judging by her face. If there's millions involved in this case and it goes in Xenon's favour, Tankersley could be ruined. That's enough of a motive. And we've only got his wife's word on the alibi."

"Fascinating," David responded. "There's the beginning of that report on Stuart's computer as well. Perhaps, on reflection, Stuart thought it was best to give the case to his partner – to avoid any personal bias. That's why he e-mailed Daniel Allgrove and began a report that he could hand over to his partner!" He peered at Jim and added, "Time we paid Robert Tankersley another visit."

They both grabbed jackets and made for the door.

They found Robert Tankersley working at home and, in the lounge, they asked him if he wanted to add anything to his previous statements.

"How do you mean?" Robert Tankersley barked.

Sitting out of sight, half-way up the stairs, Ali knew that she should retire to her room so that she would not overhear the interview. Yet it was too good an opportunity. She could not turn her back on it. Feeling guilty and hardly daring to breathe, she snooped on her own father.

"We have information that suggests you and Stuart Burrage found yourselves in opposite corners."

"What are you talking about?"

"Xenon Computing versus Megaware. And Megaware's relationship to your Alpha Systems."

Ali heard the detective's speculation about why her dad and Stuart Burrage had argued. Then she heard her father sigh loudly and confirm it in a weary voice. He admitted that it was very likely that Xenon would have its pound of flesh from him.

"But," he stressed, "that's all there is to it. I bore him a grudge, I guess. It doesn't make me a killer, you know."

"So where were you on Saturday afternoon? Not shopping with your wife," David suggested.

"No. I was here. Simple as that. Pottering in the garden. As a precaution, I got Myra to say I was with her."

Sternly, DI Thompson growled, "It's called perverting the course of justice. A serious offence. It could land you both in jail."

"Look," Robert Tankersley declared, "we're not really like this. Especially not Myra. But we were scared when Ali told us the news. We may have lied, but that's all."

Shortly after, the police officers left and Ali padded upstairs. As far as the detectives were concerned, her dad had become a key suspect. As far as she was concerned, he was already a murderer. He was a murderer because his computer chips killed people. But killing Kieran's dad with his own hands – with a knife? It seemed too close and messy.

His chips were weapons of death but the killing was well down the line, elsewhere. It was hard to imagine him wielding a knife as a weapon of death. Even so, she sat on her bed and trembled for a while. Trembled with fear and anxiety. She knew that he loved his business and she was no longer sure how far he would go to protect it.

Later on Thursday, Ali and Kieran had plenty to talk about. Kieran broke the news about the videos and Ali told him about her dad's revelations. "That's Rhia out of the picture," Ali concluded, "and Dad way up there." She grimaced.

Kieran frowned and mumbled, "Maybe."

Ali peered at him. "What's that supposed to mean?" she asked. "Rhia's got an alibi and Dad hasn't."

Kieran shrugged. "They didn't find any fingerprints, you know. The police reckon whoever did it wore gloves, but there *is* an alternative explanation." Before Ali could interrupt, he added, "And when I got back on Monday, Rhia's coat was slung over the chair."

"So?"

Kieran remarked, "It was blue."

"Yes?"

"At Heathrow, she had a white one on."

Ali stared at him. Incredulous, she exclaimed, "Good grief, Kieran! You should know Rhia by now.

She changes coats at the drop of a hat. Every time she stands in front of a different coloured wallpaper she has to change to look her best. She changed between the airport and here. That's all."

"She was wearing a green dress in Paris. I've never seen it before."

"So what? She wears a new outfit every day! You know that. She bought herself a new number in Paris, I should think."

"Yeah," Kieran replied. "I guess so."

"Besides, she was in Paris, Kieran. I know you don't like to let little things like facts get in the way of your imagination, but you can't deny she's got a terrific alibi."

"Cast-iron," Kieran muttered. As he admitted it, he was wondering if that green dress was in her wardrobe right now. If it were, and if it bore a French label, it would wrap up her perfect alibi. If it wasn't there, Kieran believed that something would not quite add up.

"I'd best get home," Ali proclaimed. "Not a pleasant prospect, but they'll get worried if I don't turn up soon." She groaned as if home had become unbearable. "You know, I really didn't think Dad was a serious suspect, but now..."

Kieran took her hand. "This is crazy," he remarked with a faint smile. "You're pointing the finger at your dad and discounting Rhia. Me, I'm the other way round. Do you think, when you live with someone, familiarity *does* breed contempt?"

Ali murmured, "Let's hope that's all it is."

They hugged each other and kissed briefly, too distracted by events and possibilities to put passion into it. Promising to get together again tomorrow, they parted.

Sleeping was not getting any easier. Kieran tossed and turned in his sweat-soaked bed. The night was muggy and Kieran's brain was overactive. He tried to relax, to concentrate on nothing at all, but thoughts rushed immediately into the vacuum. Physically, he was tired but, much to his annoyance, his mind would not leave him in peace. To himself, he muttered, "This is boring. I might as well be up, doing something."

He got out of bed and pulled on some shorts and a T-shirt. Deciding to get some fresh air into his lungs, he left his stale bedroom and crept quietly downstairs. He unlocked the back door and stood for a moment on the step, breathing deeply. It was a quiet, empty and attractive night. He could see two full moons. One was low in the sky in front of him. The other was a virtual image on the surface of the pool. It was a harmless night so he ambled into the garden.

The figure halted by the hedge that separated Kieran's back garden from the quiet street.

Convinced that no one was watching, the intruder squeezed into the secluded garden through the laurels. It was a hot night but the cloaked and hooded figure seemed to be dressed for winter. Stealthily, the stranger headed for the swimming pool where Kieran, in shorts and shirt, strolled. Without wind, the water was perfectly still, making a brilliant mirror for the moon. Keeping out of Kieran's sight, the uninvited guest crept up behind him.

Kieran sighed with relief. The air had banished his morbid imagination and put him in a better frame of mind. He had no doubt that, when he went indoors, luxurious sleep would come. For a few minutes more, though, he wanted to take in the tranquillity. There in the garden, he could be the last person on earth, untroubled by the hustle and bustle that surrounded both life and death. By the side of the pool, he stretched and then began to saunter towards the back door.

Suddenly, someone leapt at him. For an instant, Kieran saw a cloaked figure like a vampire and a lunging knife. Instinctively, he ducked and shrieked. The knife, aimed at his neck, flashed past his eyes and the intruder slammed into him. Kieran grabbed hold of his assailant and frantically held away the arm that wielded the knife. He couldn't see the face of the attacker but he had the strength of a man, he was taller than Kieran and he grunted with a deep male voice. Slowly, Kieran realized that he could not hold his arm for long. The man was stronger. The knife was getting closer to his face. Again, he cried out.

In the struggle, the man's hood fell back. The moonlight revealed an almost bald head and a face that Kieran did not recognize. "No!" Kieran bawled as the blade came within centimetres.

For a second, the intruder was distracted as Rhia appeared at an upstairs window and yelled, "What's going on?"

Kieran took the opportunity. He realized that the man would regain the upper hand at any moment, but he could tip the balance. There was one place in which he would have a natural advantage. He twisted and, still holding his attacker, threw himself into the pool. Both of them splashed into the water.

Underwater, Kieran was in his element. He could hold his breath for two whole minutes. He grasped his attacker and prevented him reaching the surface. Kieran kept a firm grip on the man till he stopped struggling. Then, freeing himself, Kieran kicked hard, still underwater. It served to propel him away from his assailant and winded the man at the same time. The knife glinted in the water as it sank to the bottom. In the rippling water, it looked like a weaving silver fish.

Kieran surfaced and realized that the stranger

was in trouble. His coat, heavy with water, was dragging him down. He spluttered and gasped for air. Kieran swam to the edge of the pool and got out. He waited till the man had ceased thrashing about like a hooked fish, then he reached out and dragged his limp body, no longer a threat, to the side. Steeling himself, he heaved the man out of the pool. The intruder collapsed helplessly at the edge. Kieran knew exactly what he should do. He'd been trained in lifesaving. But he hesitated. He found it difficult to summon the desire to revive a man who had just tried to kill him.

Above him, Rhia stammered, "Are you all right?" She clutched his shoulder.

Recovering from the shock of her appearance, he uttered, "Yeah. I'm fine. But..." He pointed to the culprit-turned-victim and said, "He needs help."

Rhia groaned but got down on her hands and knees anyway. Efficiently, she adjusted the man's position and opened his mouth to check for obstructions. "A long time ago," she said, "I trained as a nurse." Then she started resuscitation. Between mouthfuls of air, she croaked, "I've called the police, by the way."

Kieran watched as Rhia inflated the man's watery lungs, again and again. By the time that he began to gurgle, gag and breathe again, sirens were spoiling the silence of the night.

Jim arrived in the second car. He glanced

contemptuously at the sodden figure lying in the recovery position beside the swimming pool, and then turned towards Kieran. "Did you escape unscathed?"

Kieran nodded. "Who is he?"

"Don't you know?" he queried. Seeing Kieran's blank look, he pronounced, "This sad specimen is John Evans. A surgeon your dad put away for murder fifteen years ago. Our chief suspect. On a mission to eliminate the Burrage family, it seems." He turned briefly to the uniformed police officers and asked, "Searched him for weapons?"

"Yes. He's clean."

With a wry smile, he said, "He would be after taking a dip." Jim peered into the pool and enquired, "Is the knife in there?"

Kieran answered, "Yes. He dropped it when I dragged him in."

"OK," Jim said to the other officers, "who's going to get their kit off and salvage it?"

"I'll do it," Kieran volunteered. "I can't get any wetter. And I know where it went down."

Jim refused his help. "Only joking. Forensic will sort it out. We can't do their job for them. Let's get you inside, dried off, and then I'll need a statement." To his colleagues, he said, "Take Evans back to the station. Get the doctor to look at him and certify him fit to face some questions – and charges of murder and attempted murder."

As Evans was dragged to his feet, he stared at Kieran with wild eyes and uttered, "I'll be back. I'll get you Burrages yet! I'm going to wipe you all from the face of the earth." It was plain that resentment had been eating into him for years until nothing was left but insanity.

Jim grimaced with disdain and cried, "Take him away."

6

"It's all over," David informed Rhia on Friday morning. The detective was positively purring over the news. "Evans confessed. He ... er ... even bragged about it." He shook his head sadly. "Hate's been welling up in him for a long time. Not even satisfied with murdering Stuart, he'd set himself a bigger task, I'm afraid. If Kieran hadn't foiled him, he would've probably come for you next, Rhia. He destroyed his own family. Last night he wanted to finish off yours as well. He admitted it during questioning. His own family life was a disaster and now he says God whispers in his ear, telling him to devastate other families – starting with the Burrages. In other words, he's flipped. At least you can rest assured that he's locked up."

In her armchair, Rhia smiled weakly. "Yes," she said. "I feel a bit better now you've caught him. Somehow, I think I can begin to build my life again." She looked more relaxed than at any time since her husband's death.

David Thompson was preoccupied with Rhia but he did recognize Kieran's presence. The police officer glanced at him and checked, "Are you over last night's ordeal?"

"Yes," Kieran mumbled tersely.

"Good idea to dunk him in the pool. Saved your skin, I should think. Well done." He turned his attention back to Rhia.

Kieran's mind drifted. The case had been closed but his mind was still open. If Evans had killed his father, there were three things that Kieran did not understand.

Over a sandwich in the coffee bar, Kieran related last night's arrest to Ali and aired his reservations.

Once she had absorbed the shock of Evans' attack on her boyfriend and recovered from the news, she remarked contentedly, "That's it, then." She was relieved because Kieran was out of danger and because it meant that her own father could not have committed the murder. "Suddenly, it's all over. Just like that."

Kieran hesitated and sipped his coffee before questioning, "Is it?"

"What do you mean?" Ali whispered as if Kieran

were doubting the law of the land. "Evans has admitted it, hasn't he? That's what you said."

"Yes. That's what Thompson said. But when Evans was dragged away last night, he'd cracked. Totally. He was mad enough to claim that he assassinated Kennedy, as well as Dad."

"Hang on," Ali gasped. "Are you saying he didn't do it – despite the confession?"

"That's right. I think he was so besotted with the idea of murdering Dad that he imagines he has. He's probably proud of it as well." Noting that Ali was gazing at him incredulously, he added, "He really wanted to kill Dad but I reckon someone beat him to it. To get his own back, he had no choice – he had to go for me instead. He was deprived of Dad but he still wanted his pound of Burrage flesh. You see, if he … disposed of Dad, why did he yell, 'I'll get you Burrages yet,' last night? Sounded to me as if he'd still got a score to settle. It certainly doesn't sound like someone who's already killed a Burrage."

"Maybe not," Ali replied. "But, even so… Anyway, you reckon he was mad enough to say anything. If he's so crazy that he confessed to a murder he didn't commit, I'm sure he could suffer a slip of the tongue." She desperately wanted a neat and tidy end to the affair. She wanted Evans to be guilty. Otherwise, her dad would be back in the frame.

"All right," Kieran relented. "But what about the killer leaving evidence of the exact time of death?

Careless or convenient, would you say?"

Ali looked puzzled. "How do you mean?"

"Well, Rhia…"

Exasperated, Ali interrupted. "You're not still trying to blame Rhia!"

"Just bear with me," Kieran muttered under his breath so that no one else in the cafe could hear. "She knew she could prove she was somewhere else at that exact time. She might as well have stood in front of the video camera and waved." He paused and then added, "Another thing. Why do it in the middle of the afternoon?"

"What are you getting at?"

"Surely, any self-respecting murderer like Evans would creep about in the middle of the night, like he did last night, not in the full glare of the sun."

"You think Rhia set it up somehow at three-thirty – and left evidence of the time – because she could arrange to be seen on video in France then?"

"Precisely. It would be much trickier to guarantee an appearance on video after dark," Kieran explained.

"What are you saying, Kieran? It was Rhia and, while she was in France, she used a hit-man or something?"

Kieran shrugged. "Possibly."

Ali sighed but decided to humour him for a while. "And how would you prove she hired some assassin?"

"I've been wondering about that," he answered, "and I think I know. Why does a hit-man carry out a murder?"

"For money. At least that's how it works on the telly."

"Exactly. That's the lead. I think I know where her cheque book is. You must admit, it would be … interesting if she's made any big withdrawals recently."

"Well, it wouldn't prove anything but, yes, it'd be worrying. It *might* persuade me to take your theory seriously."

"There's the unknown dress thing as well," Kieran commented. He waved the remains of his last sandwich in the air. "Why don't you come round this afternoon and have a woman-to-woman chat with Rhia? You could ask after her now that the murderer's been caught."

For a second, Ali looked puzzled. Then her mouth opened and, feigning irritation at his cheek, she hissed, "So you can stick your nose in her wardrobe and cheque book while I keep her occupied! You want to use me as a decoy."

"I want you to come round anyway. It's no fun at home without you."

"Well…"

"Will you come?" Still she hesitated so Kieran continued, "Think of it like this. What if I'm right? Rhia killed him to get her hands on his money. If that's right – if she's a killer – will she want to share her new-found wealth with me?"

Startled by the thought that Kieran could be the next target, Ali submitted. "There's a lot of ifs in there but, OK, I'll come back with you. Just in case. I think you're barking up the wrong tree altogether, though." Her mind flitted impulsively to her father.

Kieran reached across the table and squeezed her hand. "Thanks. I know you don't agree with me – but that doesn't stop you helping out."

Ali added, "There's a condition. If you don't find anything while I'm doing your dirty work, distracting her, you give up this crazy notion about her."

Kieran nodded. "It's a deal," he declared.

Kieran found Rhia in the study. She was standing still, gazing wistfully at the family tree. Seeing him out of the corner of her eye, she turned towards him. She shook her head mournfully. "You know," she explained in a demure voice, "I was just wondering if I ought to have this ... updated now that we ... no longer have your father. It would acknowledge his passing. And it would be my way of finally admitting that he's gone." She wiped her eyes and asked, "What do you think?"

Kieran shrugged. "If you like." Unlike Rhia, he'd never taken an interest in family lines. It always struck him as a rather snobbish pursuit.

"Perhaps I will, then," she murmured, "but not

just now. It's too much like rubbing him out."

Kieran nodded and then announced, "Ali's come. She's in the lounge. OK?"

Rhia pulled herself together. "Oh. I'd better come and say hello to her."

While Ali diverted Rhia with small talk, Kieran excused himself for a few minutes. First, he crept back into the study. This time, he had the luxury of daylight for his exploration. As quietly as he could, he opened the filing cabinet. It groaned as if loath to yield to him but, in the day, the sound seemed much more subdued than it did in the middle of the night. His fingers flicked through the files. He came across two different cheque books. One named Rhia alone and the other was for a joint account. The counterfoils of both cheque books revealed that small sums only had been paid out recently. Kieran mumbled a curse to himself and carefully closed the drawer.

Next, he tiptoed upstairs. Rhia's room was directly above the lounge so he knew that he'd have to avoid making any noise. Cautiously, he stepped into the bedroom that had once belonged to both his real parents. Then, it smelled faintly of his mum's cosmetics. Once Rhia had reformed his dad, it smelled of his after-shave and deodorant, Rhia's perfume and the herbs that Rhia placed in a bowl on her dressing table. Now, the sole fragrance was Rhia's. Kieran made straight for her wardrobe. The door, a full-length mirror, slid back silently to display a treasure-trove of clothes. One by one, he parted and inspected the garments, like searching through the papers in the filing cabinet. It was a dazzling spectrum of expensive skirts, blouses, suits, trousers, dresses and coats. Mainly blues, reds and whites. There were just a few green items but nothing like the dress that he had seen in the video. When he drew back the mirrored door, he saw a smile on his own face. Admittedly, he'd drawn a blank with the cheque books but the dress was still a tempting mystery.

Before he left the room, he glanced round it once more and felt an immense sadness. When he witnessed Rhia's expensive clothes and her jewellery, now lying idle on the dressing table, he saw only the profits of his mother's cancer. The compensation for her death paid for Rhia's extravagance. Kieran resented every trinket and every garment, bought with a bit of his mother's life.

When he returned to the lounge, Rhia said, "Are you feeling unwell, Kieran? You seem a bit peaky."

"Yes," he answered. "I ... er ... I guess I'm still feeling the after-effects of last night. Nothing to worry about, though."

Startling them all, the telephone rang insistently. Still standing by the door, Kieran was the nearest and so he answered it. A female voice asked, "Is Rhia there?"

"Yes," Kieran muttered. "Just a minute." He held out the phone to his stepmother.

"Who is it?" she enquired.

Kieran covered the mouthpiece. "No idea. I didn't recognize the voice. A woman."

Rhia frowned. "All right. I'll take it." She took the handset from him.

Kieran and Ali sat in silence while Rhia announced herself and then went quiet for a while, listening to the caller. When she spoke again, she said, "Thanks. Yes, it's been ... trying, unpleasant, but I'm getting over it now." There was a pause before she added, "Yes. Kieran's here. We keep one another company. It helps with the shock when there's someone else around." After another brief hush, she said, "Yes. Very soon. I'm sure I'll be able to arrange it soon." She breathed her goodbye and replaced the receiver. On her way back to her seat, she declared, "Another friend, wanting to offer condolences." She acted as if she were obliged to explain the telephone call. She hesitated before commenting, "And she was asking when the funeral's going to be. You're going to have to prepare yourself for it as well, Kieran. David Thompson told me they'll let us bury him soon. I'll have to put my mind to the arrangements."

Kieran grimaced. It wasn't a pleasing prospect.

Later, when they went out on their own, Ali asked,

"Well? What did you find? Anything?"

Kieran grumbled, "I don't know what the going rate is for a hit-man, or whether you have to pay before or after, but she's not taken out a cheque for more than five hundred in the last few weeks."

"Nothing there, then," Ali concluded. "What about the dress?"

"That's the good news. It's not there. No sign of it at all," he said brightly. "She hasn't got a green dress like the one I saw her in."

"So, she didn't like it after all and threw it out. You know what she's like. Easy come, easy go."

"Yes, but you might be wrong. The lack of that dress *is* evidence. I don't know what of, to be honest. It doesn't make sense. But it's good evidence," Kieran observed.

"Hardly," Ali retorted. "Perhaps the outfit's in the wash – or at a laundry."

"Maybe," Kieran responded in a dour tone. He didn't know how to interpret the absence of the green dress, yet he still tried to convince himself that it was significant. Deep down, though, he realized that he had nothing to go on and that Ali's explanations were much more likely.

"It's not enough, Kieran. Drop it. You promised."

It had been easy to promise before the experiment. Now, after failing to find evidence of a big pay-off, Kieran was reluctant to ditch his theory. Science lessons had taught him that facts and the results of experiments should shape theories. When the facts didn't fit the theory, it was the theory that had to go. He knew it was wrong to ignore the facts and cling to a discredited theory but he didn't have the detachment of a scientist. He had confidence in his intuition. He could not admit that his confidence might be misplaced. Frustrated, he grunted his unwilling agreement to appease Ali, but he hoped that he would stumble across some other facts that would resurrect his pet theory.

7

A week later, after training, several members of the club were stuffing themselves with carbohydrate in the café, replenishing lost energy. Ali nudged Kieran and whispered, "Grit your teeth. Grin and bear it. Here comes Mike."

The backstroker, slowly increasing his swimming sessions after his widely advertised shoulder injury, wandered up to them and uttered, "How are you guys?"

Neither Ali nor Kieran made a coherent reply but their shared indistinct murmur seemed to satisfy Mike. He plonked himself down and began to chatter. It did not take him long before he began to improvise on his favourite theme. "I was with this terrific girl a couple of weekends back," he enthused. "I meant to tell you. Hair like a shampoo advert. Face like a toothpaste ad. Figure like ... a slimming advert."

Ali interjected, "What was her brain like?" She tapped the side of her head.

"Brain? Er…" He hadn't even considered it.

"And what was her name?"

"Um…" Mike thought about it for a second and then dismissed her question. "Can't remember."

Grinning, Kieran said to Ali, "You're putting him off."

"Oh, that's right," Ali replied. "Sorry, Mike. You were telling us a story."

"Yeah. But if you don't want…"

"No," Ali interrupted. "We're champing at the bit, aren't we, Kieran?"

"Sure," Kieran muttered disinterestedly.

"Good. We went for a lunchtime drink or two or three, me and ... this girl. After, when we'd had a few, we went…" He paused before adding, "That reminds me. When we were hanging round outside the pub, as you do, I saw her."

"Who?"

"Your stepmother," Mike said to Kieran.

"Rhia?" Kieran queried, suddenly attentive.

"Yes, Rhia. Anyway," Mike continued impatiently, "she was a bit merry, this girl, and…"

Kieran interrupted. "When was this?"

"Saturday afternoon."

"Which Saturday?"

"Last but one."

"Saturday the twenty-third?" Kieran checked.

"I suppose so. Yes," Mike answered.

"Where was this?"

"In town, outside the Rose and Crown."

"Did you say anything to her?"

"No, I had better things to do – concentrating on that girl. Besides, she was in a car, waiting for the lights to change."

"What sort of car?"

"Er... A white Toyota, I think. Why the grilling?"

"Nothing. It doesn't matter," said Kieran, glancing significantly at Ali.

Mike continued his far-fetched saga about the nameless beauty but Kieran did not really listen. He was itching to escape Mike's clutches and talk over the new baffling piece of evidence that had suddenly emerged.

As soon as Mike finally left them, Kieran leaned over the table and whispered urgently, "What do you make of that then?"

"I think he's a complete prat. But I guess the world would be duller without him," Ali replied. "I do wonder what'll happen when he meets a girl he's serious about, though."

"No," Kieran gasped. "I meant what he said about Rhia."

"You're not taking that seriously, are you?" Ali

uttered in amazement. "No chance. What do you believe? The videos and your own eyes or Mike's drunken fancy? Besides, I bet he hardly knows Rhia. He's probably only seen her a couple of times. He may have spotted someone who looks like her. There must be plenty of candidates with a passing resemblance to Rhia. And he said she was in a car. Tricky to see drivers clearly, I'd say." Ali hesitated and then commented, "She hasn't got a white Toyota anyway, has she?"

"No," admitted Kieran. "But it's possible to hire cars, you know."

"Yes, but would you call Mike a reliable witness, even when he's sober?"

"No," Kieran moaned. "I suppose not. But..."

"It doesn't add up, Kieran. She was in France and you know it," Ali snapped. "You promised to drop this idea."

Kieran exhaled noisily and then nodded. "Yes, I know. Guess I'm just clutching at straws."

Ali threw her arms round him and whispered in his ear, "Forget it. She's in the clear. Innocent. Even if you're right that it wasn't Evans, it's more likely to be my dad. He's got a motive and no alibi."

Kieran yielded to her common sense. Privately, though, he knew that his theory would continue to nag at him.

Kieran was surprised at the considerable hole that

his father had left. It wasn't his absence that weighed so heavily. After all, Kieran was used to his dad's absence. Even when he'd been at home, he was usually working in the study – absent to Kieran. No. It was something else. It was the atmosphere. Home life had ceased to revolve around the needs of his father. There was a void. And his dad's influence no longer diluted the effect of Rhia. Once, Kieran could eat in silence, allowing his father and Rhia to chat between themselves. Now, if there was to be conversation, and politeness demanded it, he had to engage with Rhia.

For her part, Rhia talked to him much more than she did before her husband's murder. She also began to take up her social life again. She had been to the Bridge Club a couple of times but had burst into tears on the first occasion. Her second attempt was more successful. She didn't join in. She just watched awkwardly. She was not yet ready to think about a new partner. Her housekeeper did the mundane shopping but once or twice Rhia ventured into the best shops in the city to buy those special things that made her happy. Clothes and shoes mainly. She had her hair styled and began to apply make-up again. Once more, her eyes would glitter whenever she spotted a plush, expensive car.

The police released Stuart's body and Rhia had to cope with the funeral arrangements. She found herself in communication again with her circle of friends. She even began to talk about Stuart without flinching. Her friends started to come to the house without displays of acute embarrassment at her loss. Daniel Allgrove paid two visits. The first one was an official appointment to explain Stuart's will. It was too simple to take long. Basically, he had left everything to Rhia. When Kieran reached the age of eighteen years, a quarter of his father's estate would pass to him. He would take control of another quarter if and when he married. It was understood that, eventually, on Rhia's death, the other half would follow suit. Daniel's second visit had none of the starchiness of the first. It was purely social and he offered to help with the organization of the funeral.

The funeral itself was a dour affair. Kieran had to take a prominent place alongside Rhia and he hated every moment. He felt as if he were on show before all of his father's acquaintances. It seemed that he was presenting himself for inspection. He was expected to show dignity without coldness, remorse without melancholy. Even with Ali's support, he felt unable to deliver. He didn't feel brave or devastated. He felt empty, that's all. Maybe cheated as well, but he'd been cheated long before his father had died. Now, he wondered if his dad was also being cheated. He was not sure that the police had arrested the right person.

In the graveyard, he sneaked a glance at the

massed ranks of refined mourners. David Thompson represented the police. He looked suitably sombre. Kieran wondered if it was true what TV detectives said. The murderer always turns up for the funeral. Furtively, as the vicar recited the words that he had spoken a hundred times before, Kieran scanned the faces but he was most suspicious about the one that was covered by a discreet black veil. Of course, without knowing it, he may have just seen Rhia's accomplice. If she was behind his dad's murder, she must have had an accomplice – or paid an assassin – to put her alibi into effect. It was the only solution to the riddle of her being in Paris at the time of the murder. She ordered the killing and then made sure of her foolproof French alibi while her accomplice carried out the murder at the agreed time.

For some reason, Kieran found himself peeking at David Thompson. The detective seemed to be infatuated with Rhia. And he had been very keen to blame someone else for her husband's murder. If he had participated in the killing, it was bound to be well planned. He had inside knowledge. He would have also known that John Evans had just been released from prison and was baying for the blood of the Burrages. It would be simple to pin the crime on him. And Thompson would not question Evans' confession too closely. Maybe Rhia and Detective Inspector Thompson had some sort of pact. After a decent period had elapsed, maybe they would get together. Kieran would then be living with two killers. He shuddered at the possibility.

Another option was Daniel Allgrove. An arrangement between Rhia and the lawyer was easy to imagine. Rhia had inherited the money and Daniel Allgrove had inherited the business. Mutual benefit. Ali's father had not come to the funeral, but he was another contender. At first Kieran did not take the possibility seriously. Robert Tankersley's motive would have been to halt the prosecution of his company, but surely he would have known that the death of one barrister would not kill the case. There would always be another lawyer to take it on. But then Kieran remembered sheer spite. Robert Tankersley could have exacted revenge on Kieran's dad for abandoning friendship in favour of a lucrative prosecution.

Whichever way Kieran's thoughts turned, Rhia still occupied centre stage. She had not yet made a slip, there was no hard evidence that she was guilty, but perhaps carelessness would creep in as time went by. Kieran vowed to stay alert.

Shortly after the funeral, Rhia resumed her hectic social life. Step by step, her poise, self-indulgence and vulgarity returned. A newly acquired silver Mercedes C220 Elegance was parked in the drive like a showpiece. To Kieran, the car seemed to be an ominous statement of Rhia's class and financial independence. Within a month, the house always seemed to be teeming with her friends and increasingly Kieran felt like an outsider in his own home. Occasionally, the members of the Bridge Club would descend on the house and a smug David Thompson became Rhia's new partner. Resenting her occupation and lifestyle, Kieran spent more and more time with Ali. Once, when he and Ali walked into the lounge, Rhia was getting ready to go into the city. "Hello!" she chirped. "I'm just off." She slipped a small book into her handbag and joked, "Are you two going to be good while I'm away?"

In reply, they smiled weakly at her.

She looked sleek again, groomed to perfection. And she was festooned with jewellery. To Kieran, the ornaments were dead reminders of his mother's life. As soon as Rhia strutted out of the room, Kieran cried, "Of course!"

"What?" asked Ali.

"Well…" He didn't know how Ali would react to his thoughts but he wanted to share them with her anyway. "Did you see what she put in her handbag?"

"No. What?"

"A passbook for a building society."

"So?"

Kieran explained, "Remember I found out that she hadn't made any big payments from her cheque books? Well, they were just bank accounts. She'd keep bigger amounts in a building society, I bet. If she did pay someone, it would come out of a building society account. I didn't check that."

Ali's mouth remained open but she didn't respond straight away. After a few seconds, she stammered, "I thought you'd given up on..."

Interrupting, Kieran said, "Don't tell me you're not a bit suspicious now you've seen her remarkable recovery."

Ali shrugged. "I don't suppose I like the way she's carrying on but even so..." She did not finish because her resistance was low. She knew that Kieran had a good point.

"All I'm suggesting is that we check out her building society account."

"How?" Ali enquired. "She's got the passbook and you didn't find it last time. She must keep it somewhere else."

"True. But did you see the logo on it? It was the Westland Building Society. That's where Grant McFarlane works. Remember him?"

"Yes," Ali answered, frowning. "You saved his skin on more than one occasion at school. You're thinking he owes you one."

Grant had been bullied without mercy whenever Kieran wasn't around to afford some protection. Hating it, Grant had left school as soon as he could.

Kieran nodded with guilt written all over his face.

He did not relish asking a favour of Grant because he would feel obliged to consent. To lean on poor Grant now, reminding him of the debt, would be almost as bad as the bullying in the first place. But Kieran was desperate for information. "Yes," he mumbled. "I guess Grant could get the details from a computer at work."

"It's probably illegal," Ali suggested. "Certainly unethical."

"So is murder," Kieran responded.

They planned to bump into Grant after work on the next day.

In the café, they plied Grant with coffee and asked how he liked his work at the building society. He was still amazingly thin and weak but he was dressed smartly. He looked more assured than he had ever managed at school. "It's good," he proclaimed. "Nice people."

Ali nodded sympathetically. She could imagine that he would feel safe behind a screen. He probably wished that he had conducted the whole of his life behind a screen.

Uncomfortably, Kieran said, "You know I've got a stepmother. Rhia Burrage."

"Yes," Grant answered. "And your dad died a little while ago. I saw it in the papers. Sorry."

Kieran shrugged. "It's OK. But we're supposed to be sorting out the accounts. You know. He left a lot of his money to me but ... er ... there's a possibility that my stepmother's draining the building society account for herself when half of it's mine really."

"Oh?" Grant muttered cautiously. "You should see someone about that."

"Yes," Kieran conceded. "But before I do, I need to know if it's true. I don't want to stir it up if I'm just imagining things."

Grant glanced at Ali and she nodded as if to confirm her boyfriend's words. She did her best not to blush.

"You want me to access the account?"

"Yes."

"It's not allowed." He peered at Kieran and remembered many past favours. He added in a whisper, "But she came in yesterday." He hesitated like a doctor about to break a patient's confiden-tiality. "I had to consult the manager about it. It's not often I get asked to make out a cheque for a hundred thousand pounds."

"What?" Kieran screeched. Then, more quietly, he asked, "Are you sure? Who was it made out to?"

Grant shook his head slowly. "That I can't remember. In a day I make out lots of cheques and see lots of names."

"Could you find out?"

"I ... er ... I suppose I could. It'll be in the computer record. I shouldn't, though."

"I know," Kieran said softly. "But I'd be ever so grateful."

Grant sighed. "OK. I'll check it tomorrow," he moaned.

Ali put in, "It'd be useful to know where the cheque gets cashed as well, wouldn't it, Kieran?"

"I guess so," he agreed. Turning to Grant, he quizzed, "Can you do that as well?"

Grant was as white as he used to be when some lads approached him menacingly. He nodded. "It'll take a good few days, though. And it could be up to six months."

Kieran smiled and, to lighten the mood as well as his own conscience, he quipped, "No one waits six months to cash a cheque for a hundred thousand!"

"I suppose not," Grant whimpered.

They arranged to meet again whenever Grant had news about the destination of Rhia's cheque.

"Ali, love! Do me a favour." Her mother's voice floated in from the kitchen. "Fetch me your dad's mug, will you? He's left it in the study, I think."

"All right," Ali called out. "I'm on my way."

She dragged herself away from the television and went into the study to collect the missing mug. It was lying between the mouse mat and a small pile of computer chips. She grabbed it and turned to leave when something caught her eye. Bending down, she confirmed that her eyes weren't deceiving her. In the bin, there was a pair of thin nylon gloves that had once been white. Now, they were stained brown with dried blood. Ali stared at them and swallowed. Suddenly, she felt quite sick. There could be any number of explanations for the bloody gloves, she realized, but there was one particular explanation that petrified her.

She jumped and issued a startled cry when her mum yelled, "Can't you find it?"

"Er... Yes. Just got it." She staggered to the kitchen and handed over the mug.

"Thanks," her mum said. Then she added, "Are you feeling all right, love?"

Ali knew that her cheeks were tellingly red. She could not hide her shock but she denied it anyway. "I'm ... fine. Thought I'd go and see Kieran."

"Fair enough. Looks like you need a bit of fresh air anyway."

Kieran was taken aback by her discovery. "You think your dad was in on the murder," he surmised. Kieran had never really believed that Robert Tankersley had murdered his dad. He had no real reason to count him out but he just didn't seem the type. Even so, Kieran knew that he did have a powerful motive. Vengeance. "You think he killed Dad, wearing those gloves, kept them till the fuss died down, and now he's getting rid of them."

"It's a horrible thought," Ali replied, "but, you must admit, it could be."

"Yeah, it could be. But it's a bit careless, isn't it, just leaving them in the bin for everyone to see?"

"Hardly everyone," Ali argued. "Only me or Mum."

"Did you take one?" asked Kieran.

"No. What for?"

"I'm sure someone could check if the blood's Dad's."

"The police could," Ali agreed. "But they've shut the case."

"True. I guess you'll just have to confront him."

Ali's mouth opened. "How do you mean?" she gasped.

"Ask him about the gloves. I bet there's an innocent explanation."

"It'd be like accusing him of murder," Ali objected.

"That's exactly what you're doing," Kieran observed.

"Yes, but ..." She sighed before continuing. "Not to his face. I couldn't say anything to his face."

"You'll think of something," Kieran commented confidently.

Later that day, Ali and Kieran got together again. "Well?" Kieran prompted. "Have you got an update on the gloves?"

Ali nodded. "I found a way of doing it," she said. "I told him I'd seen the gloves when I went into the study. I asked if he'd hurt himself."

"Good tactic," Kieran muttered. "And ...?"

"He said he had. Said he was trying out new chips. He wears gloves so he doesn't get grease on them. Can be catastrophic, apparently. Anyway, he turned one over – legs in the air, as he put it – and later put his hand down heavily on it. The legs went straight through the glove and into his hand. Drew quite a bit of blood. No great harm done, he said."

"Sounds reasonable," Kieran remarked. "But," he added, "you don't look much happier. Didn't you believe him?"

"I'm not sure. I thought I knew him well enough, but perhaps I don't. Perhaps he's been lying all along and I haven't twigged. He certainly didn't volunteer to show me the wound."

"He thought it was too trivial to show off," Kieran guessed.

"I sneaked back into the study," Ali told him. "I couldn't see a chip with blood on it. It wasn't on the desk or in the bin."

Kieran shrugged. "They cost the earth, don't they? He wouldn't just chuck it. He'd clean it up and use it again."

Ali still looked worried. "I don't know. Let's hope that's the answer."

"Bound to be," Kieran replied, trying to cheer her up. He touched her shoulder gently. "Besides, there's a much more likely culprit," he murmured.

Ali peered at him. Seizing the opportunity to talk for a while about a different suspect, she said, "I've been thinking about that as well. This hit-man idea. It doesn't really work, you know."

"Why not?"

"Well," Ali deduced, "if Rhia paid an assassin to … do the job, why did she feel the need to leave the country to give herself an alibi? A bit extreme, isn't it? She could have gone to a friend's house on the appointed day – just down the road. That'd be a lot easier and give her a perfectly good alibi. Better than relying on being caught on video."

"Yes," Kieran mumbled thoughtfully. "I hadn't thought of that." He stroked his chin and then added, "It doesn't mean I'm wrong about the hit-man, but I see your point. Going to Paris is a bit over the top. If it wasn't an assassin, perhaps she had another reason for paying someone a lot of money."

He was still intrigued by Mike's unlikely sighting of Rhia in a Toyota at the same time that a video camera recorded her in Paris. He knew that it made no sense. He knew that Mike was not reliable. He knew that a drunken Mike had not seen the woman clearly. But there was just a chance that Rhia *was* near home at the time of the murder. If she had fooled the cameras somehow, she could have committed the crime herself. Maybe someone had doctored the pictures to make it seem that they were recorded on the Saturday when in fact they were

Friday's videos. Perhaps she posed in front of the cameras on Friday, bribed a security officer to interfere with the date, came back to England on the Saturday, killed her husband, and then returned to complete her trip. Then the enormous withdrawal from the building society would be the fee for tinkering with the videotape. The idea might seem absurdly complicated but Kieran decided to follow it up anyway.

When he explained his new theory to Ali, she frowned but did not try to knock it down. "So, how can you check it out?" she enquired.

"Not sure," he confessed. "But I think I'd better call a local car hire company."

Pretending that he was about to take a trip to France, he telephoned to enquire about booking a car for a day on his return to England. The assistant asked where he would enter the country. "Er ... I haven't finally decided," he answered. "It could be Heathrow or one of the ports maybe."

"Well," the woman responded, "we could have a car waiting at Heathrow for you. That's no problem. Some of the ferry terminals would be more difficult for us. You may need to contact one of the national companies. You'll find them at all major ports and the like."

"I see," Kieran said into the mouthpiece. "And if I definitely wanted a Toyota?"

"We don't deal with Toyotas at all, sir."

"Do any of those national ones?"

The woman was getting a little impatient. "Yes. Several," she answered abruptly.

"Thank you," Kieran said. "When I've sorted out exactly what I'm doing I'll call you back. Thanks again."

"You're welcome, sir," the woman replied in a tone that expertly disguised her irritation.

Kieran muttered a curse as he replaced the telephone. It was an impossible task to check every place that Rhia may have used to re-enter the country. And even if he made a lucky guess, he didn't know what name she would have used to hire the Toyota. Certainly not her own. Perhaps she'd had to pay for a forged driving licence as well.

"Oh, well," he said to Ali. "It wasn't wasted. At least we know she could've come back and hired a Toyota for the day." Even so, he was disappointed. He was forced to abandon the lead before he'd made any real progress. Instead, he had to rely on Grant tracing that cheque.

8

Kieran had to wait for ten days before he got any news from Grant. And when it came, it meant nothing to him.

Grant fidgeted with a pen and glanced round nervously before he announced, "The cheque was made out to someone called Sandra Jackson."

"Sandra Jackson?" Kieran looked blankly at Grant and then at Ali.

Ali murmured, "You don't know her?"

"No," Kieran answered. "Never heard of her."

"Where did she cash the cheque, then?" Ali asked.

"A bank in St Peter Port. High Street."

"St Peter Port?" Kieran repeated. "Where's that?"

"Guernsey. Channel Islands."

"Oh." Kieran scratched his head. Bewildered, he

said, "I don't know anyone there, that's for sure."

"Rhia does," Ali interjected.

"So it seems."

"Well…" Grant muttered. It was his reticent way of asking for their permission to escape. Clearly he wanted to put the whole illegal episode behind him. Once Kieran had thanked him and apologized for applying pressure, Grant scuttled away like a small frightened animal.

"Sandra Jackson of Guernsey," Kieran groaned. "I'm none the wiser."

"So, what do we do?"

Kieran thought about it for a few moments. Then he pronounced, "We go to the reference library and check out a Guernsey phone book."

Ali said, "Have you got any idea how many Jacksons there might be in Guernsey?"

"No," he admitted. "None at all. Let's find out."

There were thirty-nine. "A manageable number," Kieran concluded in a hushed voice.

"Manageable for what?"

In the quiet of the library, he whispered, "We'll call them all and see if we can find her. We'll start with the S. Jacksons. There's only two of them."

"Yes, but if she's married," Ali pointed out, "the number will come under her husband's initials, I should think. So it's unlikely to be S. Jackson. It could be anything."

"I know," Kieran replied. "But we've got to start somewhere."

"And what will you say if you get through to her?" Ali breathed as Kieran took the directory to the photocopier. "Hello, Mrs Jackson. Are you a paid assassin or someone who fiddles video evidence? This is the son of your last victim. Have you spent your profits yet?"

Kieran shrugged. "Look, I'll copy the page so we can take the numbers home. I doubt if Rhia will be there. She'll be out with her mates. We can use the phone in peace. There's plenty of time to work out tactics before we get home."

"You keep saying we," Ali observed.

Kieran grinned at her. "It's OK. I'll do it. But you can hold my hand."

On the way home, Kieran remarked, "I think you're right. We can forget the hit-man. Have you ever heard of a female one – hit-woman? Unlikely. But she could have helped Rhia to sneak back to England, while still appearing to be in Paris. Some sort of security expert who can doctor video equipment – so it reads the wrong date."

"Don't you think someone in Paris would've noticed that?"

"I don't know." Struggling to keep his ailing theory alive, he commented, "All I know is you can do some clever things if you've got the right equipment."

Ali was sceptical, but she didn't try to cast further doubt on his hunch. Instead, her thoughts turned to the telephone calls. "All right, but what *do* you say if you get her on the phone?"

Kieran sniffed and considered it. "Perhaps just hang up. That way, we find out how many Sandra Jacksons there are and where they live. Then we can concentrate the investigation."

"Oh, it's an investigation now, is it?" Ali taunted him. "If you think like that, you ought to go to the police."

"We can't. We'd get Grant into trouble. Besides," he explained, "knowing Dad's business from the inside taught me that the whole thing's a game. The law's there to give the impression that justice is being done, but half the time I wonder if it is. It's about winning or losing an argument in court. It's not about finding out the truth. As long as there's a culprit who can be prosecuted successfully, the law's satisfied."

"I've heard this lecture before," Ali mentioned.

"Sorry. I'm just saying that Thompson's part of the game. He's happy because he's got someone behind bars and a confession. He won't waste any more time on it. On top of that, have you seen the way he sucks up to Rhia? He seems pleased to have Dad out of the way, milking the opportunity. If he really fancies her, there's a chance he was involved. If so, he's not going to open the case again, is he?

But *I* think there's still a few question marks – a few things to investigate."

"OK, Chief Inspector Kieran Burrage. How exactly do you propose to investigate someone in Guernsey?"

"You haven't had your summer holiday yet, have you? Raid your piggy bank. I'm told the Channel Islands are nice at this time of year." Kieran grinned cheekily.

Exasperated, Ali cried, "Are you serious?"

"Yes. We can take your tent. It shouldn't be too expensive if we camp."

"And when you tell Rhia where you're going, what is she going to think?"

"Mmm." Kieran hesitated and then suggested, "There are plenty of Channel Islands, aren't there? We'll tell her we're going to one of the others."

Ali gave up objecting. She decided to take it a step at a time. There was no point worrying about a crazy scheme to go to Guernsey until Kieran had tried to trace the mysterious Sandra Jackson by phone.

His research did not get off to a flying start. Dialling the first S. Jackson elicited the number unobtainable tone and the second one connected him with a sullen man called Steven. Having failed with the S. Jacksons, Kieran began to go through the other Jacksons in alphabetical order. His third call quickened his heart rate. "Is Sandra there, please?" he asked.

The female voice on the line sounded surprised and suspicious. "Sandra? You want Sandra?"

"Yes, please."

"On the phone?" the woman queried. "Are you sure?"

"Yes," Kieran uttered.

"Well, she's fast asleep and she wouldn't say much to you anyway."

"Oh. Why not?"

The woman's tone had changed. She almost seemed amused. "Because she's three months old."

"Ah. I see," Kieran stammered. "Sorry. I must have the wrong Sandra Jackson."

There was a chuckle on the line. "I think so. I'll tell her you called, if you like, but I doubt if she'll call back for a few years."

"Sorry," Kieran repeated.

"That's OK. It's cheered me up."

The telephone clicked and Kieran murmured, "Oops!" After he'd explained the call to Ali and endured more giggles at his expense, he tried more numbers and drew more blanks.

His enthusiasm for the task was beginning to wane when he had a lucky break. In response to Kieran's enquiry, the man on the other end of the line said, "No. She's out. She'll be back in about half an hour. Who is this?"

"It doesn't matter," Kieran replied. "I'll call back." With a hand that trembled, he put down the receiver as if it were red hot. "Phew! Got one!" he cried to Ali. He ran his finger down the list of Jacksons in the directory. "This one, it was. Listed as J.A. Jackson." He marked the entry with a cross. "She lives in St Peter Port as well. Handy for the bank," he remarked. "I'm going to have a quick rest. I don't suppose you want to...?"

Ali's firm shake of the head stopped him finishing his question. "It's your show," she said, refusing the telephone. "Your privilege." For a moment she considered him as he sat back in the easy chair, recovering from the shock of success. "You know," she said sadly, "I don't think I'd heard you lie till this investigation of yours. You lied to Grant. You're lying to these people on the phone, and you're proposing to lie to Rhia if you go to Guernsey. I know why you're doing it but don't make a habit of it, will you? I hate to see you getting good at it. I don't want you to lie to me – ever."

Kieran leaned forward and touched her leg. "Not to you, I won't. I'm not enjoying it, you know. It's just till I get to the bottom of Dad's death."

"As long as you can stop when it's over. I don't want you addicted to it like Mike. I'll want honest Kieran back again."

"You'll have him soon enough. But for now..." With a weary sigh of uneasiness, he picked up the receiver once more.

He discovered only two more Sandra Jacksons.

Judging by the young voice, one was perhaps ten or eleven years old. Kieran noted from the list of names, addresses and telephone numbers that she lived in St Saviour. He marked the entry but discounted any notion that she was both a crook and the lucky recipient of one hundred thousand pounds.

For the final time, he asked, "Is Sandra Jackson there?"

"Speaking." This time it was a woman's voice.

Thinking quickly, Kieran feigned surprise. "Oh!" he uttered. "Sorry but ... er ... you don't sound like the Sandra I was expecting. I'm calling to wish her a happy eleventh birthday. I must have the wrong Sandra Jackson."

The woman, sounding distrustful, muttered, "You sure have."

"Sorry," Kieran replied. He hung up. Turning to Ali, he declared, "That's the lot. Four Sandra Jacksons. Two underage and probably out of it. That last one lives in..." He scanned the directory and then added, "St Martin." While he highlighted the entry, he asked, "Is that near St Peter Port?"

"I think everywhere's close to St Peter Port on Guernsey. It's not a big place."

"And is everywhere called Saint something?"

Ali shrugged. "Sounds like it. But I guess you're going to drag me back to the library to find out – to look at a map," she surmised.

Kieran laughed. "You know me pretty well."

"Better than you think," she rejoined. "You're going to call in at a travel agent as well. Check out the cost of the ferry."

"No, I wasn't," Kieran said, wagging his finger at her, "but now you've suggested it..."

Ali grinned at him. "You can't fool me. You'd already thought of it."

"And you can't fool me," Kieran countered. "You're pretending you don't like the idea but really you're dying to get stuck into an investigation. You're not so laid back about it as you'd like me to think."

"All right, all right. We've proved we both know each other inside out," Ali replied, calling a truce to their banter. "If we've got to go, let's get on with it. Otherwise the travel agent's and library will be closed anyway."

Kieran put down his toast, gulped, took a deep breath and then peered at Rhia. "I ... er ... I need to get away for a bit," he proclaimed as if he were expecting an argument about it.

"Oh. What do you mean?" Rhia enquired.

Kieran's gaze reverted for a moment to the kitchen table, then he looked up resolutely. "After Dad and all. I need some time ... I don't know ... to get my head sorted out, I guess."

Even at breakfast time, Rhia was back to her most

immaculate. She beamed at him and purred, "Sounds like a good idea to me. And something tells me you'll want Ali with you."

"Yes."

"Fair enough. She's a nice girl and I'm sure the two of you will behave." Rhia picked up her cup of coffee but before she took a sip, she asked, "Where were you thinking of going?"

Brashly, Kieran answered, "The Channel Islands. Ali suggested Jersey."

Of course, it could have been a coincidence but as soon as Kieran referred to the Channel Islands some coffee slopped over the rim of her cup and splashed on to the tablecloth. It was odd because Rhia was not normally clumsy. She didn't make slips without a reason. For a split-second she glared at Kieran but by the time that he named Jersey, she had recovered her composure. Dabbing at the stain with a napkin, she said, "Jersey? It sounds nice ... but why there?"

"*Because* it sounds nice. One of Ali's mates went there last year," Kieran fibbed. "She recommended it." Her fumble when he mentioned the Channel Islands justified the lie. The fact that she had spilled a little coffee would hardly stand up in court as evidence but, in Kieran's eyes, the jolt condemned her. She had been startled. More than ever, he was convinced that she had something to hide.

On reflection, he believed that he'd been right to

announce his departure to the Channel Islands before he'd mentioned Jersey. It had allowed him to observe her reaction. Yet he was also aware of the peril. The woman sitting opposite him might have just realized that he suspected her. She might have guessed that he knew about the cheque. And she might have interpreted his holiday correctly as his means of investigating her. Kieran would have to watch his back from now on. He might also have to watch over Ali. Rhia would expect Kieran to share all of his thoughts and suspicions with Ali. Suddenly, both of them could have become targets.

Rhia smiled sweetly. "Excellent. It'll be good for you – both of you. I'm delighted. Whereabouts in Jersey?"

"Haven't decided yet. We'll camp so we can move around."

"Where did Ali's friend go?" Rhia persisted, as if she were testing her stepson.

"Ali knows. I'm not sure. We've still got to plan the details." It was like playing a tough game of chess, full of hidden hostility, after revealing his tactics to his opponent.

"I see." Rhia smirked. "When are you going? Where from? Have you planned that yet? And how are you getting there?"

"Next weekend. We were lucky. Some couple cancelled and we got their places on the boat at short notice. Because of that, it was cheap as well. It's just a week on Jersey. We take some sort of high-speed catamaran from Weymouth, early next Saturday morning. We'll get to Weymouth by coach the day before, I suppose." He hesitated and asked, "Have you ever been to the Channel Islands?" He tried to make it sound like a casual, innocent question.

"No. It's one of those places I've always meant to visit but never quite made it. Still," Rhia hissed, "I'm sure you'll enjoy it."

When Kieran left the table, he found that he was sweating. He had just hinted to her that he was on her trail, testing her alibi, trying to discover if and how she had committed murder. Unwisely, he had also told her his exact movements – but he had no option. He hoped that she would not check with the travel company which island was their real destination. The catamaran called at St Peter Port and then went on to Jersey, but it would do so without Kieran and Ali.

Until the weekend, he would have to live alongside a woman who might wish to dispose of him. Kieran felt nervous and uncomfortable – but safe. She would not try anything in her own house – at least not while she was around to face the accusations. Kieran believed that she had killed his father using some devious plan to avoid detection. He assumed that, if she was determined to rid herself of a threat – and an heir who would take away half of her husband's money – she would set up another intricate and ingenious scheme. Ironically, he estimated that he was not in danger while he stayed close to her. At the same time, he could hardly bear to be near her. He relished separation. Yet the distance could provide her with the space she needed to devise another murder and another alibi. To solve the crime, though, Kieran had to accept the risk. He longed to get away to Guernsey where he felt that the answer lay.

9

"Are you OK?"

Sandwiched between their bulging haversacks, Ali and Kieran sat in the lounge of the catamaran as it surfed the Channel, crossing the busy shipping lanes, dodging the other sea craft.

"How do you mean?" Kieran replied. "Of course I'm all right. I'm on my hols, aren't I? Everyone's OK on their hols."

"Not just a holiday," Ali remarked. "Anyway, I meant you keep looking round like a spy."

"Just ... er ... eyeing up the girls," he said with a grin.

She poked him in the ribs with her elbow. "I hope you get seasick, then."

From the open sea, the huddle of buildings

growing out of the hillside looked like a toy town. Once Ali and Kieran had disembarked and walked into St Peter Port, it seemed like any other haphazard seaside town at nine-thirty in the morning. A curious mixture of locals going about their businesses and tourists beginning to clutter the narrow busy streets. The harbour road was awash with cars, taxis, delivery lorries and buses. Behind it, churches, shops, restaurants and pubs were clustered. On the pavements, blackboards announced fishing trips, guided tours, menus, special offers. In High Street, Kieran pointed to a round domed building that seemed to block the road. "That's the bank where she cashed the cheque," he remarked.

"Before we think about all that," Ali suggested, "let's establish base camp. We need to find out how to get to our site."

They bought a map from the tourist office and discovered which bus they needed to catch. It took them three miles inland and dropped them off between a wartime hospital built underground as a dismal concrete maze and a bizarre tiny chapel built from bits of broken pottery and shells. They strolled half a mile up a peaceful lane along the valley to reach the campsite. "London, it ain't," Ali observed. "Can't smell the exhaust fumes. Great!"

As soon as they had pitched the small tent, a dreary drizzle set in. They nestled inside where the rain on the taut nylon sounded like small pebbles. "I bet even the rain's clean here. It probably won't burn through the tent like the stuff at home."

After they had laid out their sleeping bags, they settled down to examine the map, made orange by the daylight piercing the fabric of the tent. Tapping the unfolded plan of the island, Kieran declared, "Doyle Road, St Peter Port. That's where one of the adult Sandra Jacksons lives." He marked it with a biro.

"Which one?"

"It's ... er ... J.A. Jackson. That's the husband, I suppose. The other one, W.A., is in St Martin. Jerbourg Road. Let's see." He peered at the names and numbers written among the tangle of lanes. "Here we are. Jerbourg Road. A number 2 bus will get us there, it says. It's not that far out of St Peter Port."

"And it's near Fermain Bay. My information says that's a really good beach," Ali hinted.

"Beach?" Kieran's mind was absorbed in other things.

"Yes," Ali cried, nudging him. "We are on our hols, remember. It's not all Jacksons and Bergerac, you know."

"Wrong island," Kieran taunted her. "Bergerac was the detective on Jersey."

"Don't try and wriggle out of it," she retorted. "Holiday equals beaches plus swimming. Look, there's a disco at Jerbourg. I'm not going to let you forget that we're here for fun as well."

Kieran smiled at her. "Sure. I know. But if we get the serious business done straight away, it leaves the rest of the week to play at tourists. Yes?"

"All right. But not now," Ali insisted. "I'm tired out after the travelling. We'll be budding Bergeracs tomorrow – especially if it's still raining. As soon as the sun comes out, though, I'm back on my hols."

As usual, Ali had the last word.

On Sunday, the two of them stood, feeling damp, foolish and unnerved, on one side of Doyle Road and gazed across at the Jacksons' house. It was a terraced property, small and neat. A ramp led up from the garden to the front door.

"Well?" Ali prompted.

"Mmm. It isn't exactly what I expected for someone who's just banked a hundred thousand."

"No," Ali agreed. "The thing is, though, are we going to loiter here till the police take us away – on the off-chance that Sandra Jackson will come out like the prime minister to make a statement?"

"No, I guess not. But first we ought at least to get a look at her." Kieran pondered on it for a moment. He put his arm round Ali in the vain hope of buttering her up and said, "Back home, do you get visits from those religious nuts? You know, they always come in pairs like police officers and one asks if you've read the Bible lately and would you like to discuss your feelings about it. The other just stands there and smiles. Yes?"

Ali closed her eyes and moaned. "That's your plan, is it, to get her to the door?" She shook her head. "You want us to pay a doorstep visit to talk about the Bible. What happens if she says yes?"

"No one says yes. We'll be safe. But I don't know what we do after. Let's take it a step at a time, though."

"And which is my role?"

Kieran squeezed her shoulders and grinned at her. "Just put on your best silly smile. Think of something nice while I talk."

"Tricky. I'll be shaking like a leaf," Ali answered. "We might be about to crash in on a hired assassin."

"You're exaggerating," Kieran complained. "We don't really believe the assassin story. Remember?" To lighten the burden, he added, "It's more likely to be someone who forges documents and manipulates video pictures."

"Still an accomplice, though. Anyway, if we're going to do it, let's get it done before I lose my nerve altogether."

Kieran pressed the door bell, breathed deeply, and waited. His pulse raced as if he'd just swum two hundred metres flat out. Ali's fixed expression was half-way between ecstasy and fright.

It was a man in his fifties that fumbled with the

131

door catch and then appeared, a puzzled look on his face. "Yes?" he muttered.

"Good morning," Kieran responded in his best far-away tone. "We wondered if you had read the Bible recently and what you gained from it. What feelings did you have about it?"

Mr Jackson sighed. "My feelings would be unrepeatable, young man."

Behind him, there was a dingy hall and some sort of contraption at the bottom of the staircase.

Before Kieran could reply, there was a voice from inside. "Who is it?"

The old man turned and called back into the house, "It's them religious folk, telling us that the world's going to be perfect and free of suffering if only we follow the way of Jesus. Do you want to have a word, Sandra?"

"Yes," came the shouted reply.

Mr Jackson said, "Hang on a moment."

Kieran and Ali glanced at each other, barely able to sustain their smiles.

Mr Jackson withdrew into the hall and opened the door to the living room. Eventually, a woman in a wheelchair emerged, turned on the spot and headed for the front door. Kieran and Ali stopped smiling and simply looked ashamed.

Sandra Jackson examined the two callers and uttered, "Does your God, your Jesus, prevent suffering? Can He cure me? Can He take away arthritis?" She held out her hands, the wrists and knuckles deformed and useless.

Kieran felt sure that the real door-to-door evangelists would have a stock answer, but he had nothing to offer.

Sandra Jackson stared at them and then cackled, "No wonder you look guilty. If you don't mind, I'll pass on your perfect world." She closed the door on them before they could apologize, deeply embarrassed by the whole episode.

Despondently, they walked back towards the centre of the town. "Well," Kieran muttered, trying to break the black mood, "at least we can strike her off the list."

"Yes," Ali replied. "I hope we didn't upset her. Did you see her hands? They were ... mangled, really. It was awful."

"Horrible," Kieran agreed. "She's no assassin, that's for sure. And she's not up to anything that needs skilful hands, either."

"Poor woman," Ali murmured, still feeling sheepish about their blundering.

Recognizing that it was not a good time to propose that they should seek their second candidate, Kieran suggested instead that they should look around the castle next to the quay, followed by a thrash in the sea. Ali glanced at him with relief and gratitude.

"Thanks," she said, interlocking her arm with

his. "Anything but more police work. I couldn't face another one like that just yet. Playing at tourists will put it out of my mind."

The following morning, Kieran attempted to sweeten Ali. Gently, he asked if she wanted the promised visit to Fermain Bay and the Jerbourg area, ending the day with the disco.

She saw straight through his suggestion, of course. "You mean, you want to chase up the next Sandra Jackson and make it up to me by having a bit of time on the beach like ordinary folk?" She paused and then murmured her assent. "Let's do the private detective bit first. I might need the beach and a dance to make me feel better afterwards."

Their first bus of the day took them into St Peter Port and the second meandered towards Jerbourg and St Martin's Point. Jerbourg Road was quite long and, from the bus, they could not locate the Jacksons' house. They alighted and walked until they arrived at the right number. It was a bungalow. The last in a row of cottages that had seen better days. The garden gate dragged on the path and Kieran had to lift it to open it properly.

"Same again?" he whispered to Ali. "Put on your best smile." He banged on the front door and waited. And waited. Then he banged again. "You know, I've got a bad feeling about this," he breathed. "I don't think there's anyone home." He used the knocker for the last time and then lifted the letter-box and peered into the bungalow. "Seems deserted," he concluded.

Ali sighed. "Now what?"

Kieran peered about. There was no one in sight. "We could walk round the back. Just in case she's in the back garden."

Ali did not like the sound of it but she did not want to have to return on another day. "Come on, then," she replied.

Feeling like crooks, they slipped down the side of the cottage and sneaked into the rear garden. It was well tended but also deserted. The second grown-up Sandra Jackson was proving elusive.

"Now we're here, I could take a look through the window." He stepped over a flower-bed and on to the patio. Pressing his face up to the glass and cutting out the reflections with his hand, he gazed into the living room. It was nothing special. Kieran expected it to be old-fashioned but the colours were modern and bright. A small neat room.

Suddenly, Kieran gasped and Ali whispered urgently, "What is it?"

Kieran beckoned to her. "Come and take a peek. Tell me if I'm dreaming or not. Over there," he said, pointing. "On the shelf."

Ali squinted and then uttered, "Good grief! You're not dreaming." When she stared at her boyfriend her face was white. "What does it mean?"

"I don't know. Why should she have a framed photo of Rhia in her living room?"

Still not quite believing it, they peered through the window again.

Both of them leapt and banged their heads on the glass when, behind them, a voice said pointedly, "Can I help you?"

Rubbing their foreheads, they turned. A burly man with a spade in his hands stood there. They were not sure if the spade was a weapon or whether he had just been doing some gardening. "You startled us," Kieran stuttered. "Are you Mr W. Jackson?"

The man frowned. "No," he snapped, examining them with curiosity and distrust. "I'm the next-door neighbour and you look like prowlers to me." Menacingly, he adjusted his grip on the spade.

"No," Kieran replied, trying to be nonchalant. "We're just looking for Sandra. We knew her quite well a while ago. She gave us her address and told us to drop in. We were in the area so we thought we'd pay her a surprise visit, but she doesn't seem to be in."

The neighbour hesitated. He seemed less hostile once Kieran had proved that he knew Sandra's name. Somehow, it made his explanation more believable. "You didn't know her husband, though, and you're not from round here."

"Er ... no. We're from England – and we only met Sandra."

"Mmm," the man mumbled. "How long is it since you've been in contact?"

"Months," Kieran lied. "Last year some time, I think."

"That explains it," he said, relaxing somewhat. He rested the spade on the patio. "She went on holiday on Friday. Asked me to keep an eye on the property."

"Is she taking a break on Guernsey?"

"No. Said she was off to London."

"And her husband?" asked Kieran.

The man shook his head sadly. "Died. If you'd been local, you'd know."

"Oh, I'm sorry to hear that. When?" Kieran queried.

"Just before Christmas last."

Ali nudged her boyfriend and said, "If she's not here, we might as well get going." She wanted to escape while their luck held.

"True." Kieran thanked the neighbour and apologized for the intrusion. "Pity we missed her," he concluded. As they walked away, the man with the spade watched them. His eyes escorted them from Sandra Jackson's premises. Kieran whispered to Ali, "Don't rush. Saunter."

"I feel like running," she replied, clearly shaken by the encounter.

"Too suspicious," Kieran muttered.

Once they were back on the main road, they

scurried away as quickly as they could.

Safely on the footpath that led to Fermain Bay, they chatted about their uncanny discovery. Kieran was baffled. "What does that photo of Rhia mean?"

"No idea," Ali said. "But it tells us we found the right Sandra Jackson, even if she's not around at the moment. It tells us there *is* a Guernsey connection."

Thoughtfully, Kieran speculated, "It's quite a coincidence that she went on holiday just before we got here. I wonder if Rhia tipped her off. If Rhia realized we were on her trail and didn't want us to meet her… It's a possibility."

"And there's another coincidence," Ali put in. "Another woman with a husband who's died recently."

"Yeah. We can find out about that," Kieran replied. Reading his mind, Ali interjected, "I know. He said anyone round here would've known about it. So I bet it got in the local papers. We need a trip to yet another library – to trace the story."

"You got it," Kieran chirped. "Let's…"

Ali interrupted him immediately. "Let's enjoy the sea and sand – and the disco. The library'll be open tomorrow."

Kieran would have preferred to follow the lead straight away but he gave in. "OK. I fancy a swim, I suppose. Looks like blue sky's making a comeback as well. We did agree to ease up when the sun does its stuff."

*　　*　　*

They found the library behind the bus station. One of the assistants led them to a microfiche reader and set it up for past copies of the local newspaper. They scanned down the endless columns of articles. "Here we go," Kieran mumbled. "December issues coming up. Keep your eyes open."

Kieran scanned down them until Ali cried softly, "Hold it!"

The headline on 22nd December read, "Local man dies in drugs mix-up."

Sitting side by side, Ali and Kieran read the report. Apparently, Mr William Jackson was 45 years old and not in the best of health. He was virtually house-bound and needed daily medication. He died while his wife was away, taking a short break from caring for him. She returned to find him dead on the floor of the living room. The post-mortem and analysis of the residue of the tablets showed that he had been given the wrong ones. The police did not understand how or why his treatment had been altered and his pharmacist had no record of a change in his prescription. It was evident that someone had tampered with his supply of drugs. Clearly the authorities suspected murder more than an accident, but motive remained a mystery.

The next day's paper relegated the story to page three. Sandra Jackson had been interviewed as part of the police investigation yet had been released without charge. She had definitely been in Britain when the culprit had interfered with her husband's medication. The police also seemed satisfied that she did not have the required medical knowledge. The article concluded that the case remained open and enquiries were on-going. Ali and Kieran searched three more weeks of newspapers but did not discover any further reports. It was an unsolved crime.

They removed the microfiche, turned off the reader, and looked at each other. Ali was the first to react. "It all sounds very familiar," she commented.

Kieran nodded. "Yet more coincidences. Wife away when hubby is murdered. She returns to find him dead. The police check out her alibi but seem satisfied that she's in the clear. Miles away. Cast-iron alibi. Like Rhia's."

"I'm ... worried, Kieran. This is telling us something, but I don't know what," Ali whispered.

"Yeah," Kieran murmured. "And there's that photo of Rhia. If I didn't know that she's lived in my house for the last five years, I'd say she had a double life. She lived here as Sandra Jackson and did in her husband at Christmas with a perfect alibi, then, as Rhia Burrage, she repeated the performance on Dad."

Ali smiled and shook her head. "Yes, but..."

"I know. It's a daft idea because it's impossible."

"True," Ali said. "But do you know where Rhia

was just before last Christmas?"

Kieran inhaled and then slowly let out the breath as he thought. "Last Christmas. Well, on the day itself, she was at home. But ... er ... before it, she did go somewhere. We were deep in swimming training, Dad was working round the clock to clear the decks for Christmas, and so Rhia took herself off on one of her trips. I have a feeling she went to Edinburgh."

"What for?"

Kieran shrugged. "To do Rhia-like things, I guess. Shop a lot. Do the castle and art galleries."

"Mmm. The opposite direction from Guernsey," Ali remarked. "It's got me beat."

"Let's go down to the harbour," Kieran suggested. "We'll get a bag of unrecognizable seafood and slurp it down while we watch the boats come and go. Later, we'll find another club. Yes?"

"Agreed!"

They had a few drinks and danced until they'd missed the last bus. "Ah, well," Ali exclaimed, "Never mind. It was worth it. Good fun." A bit tipsy, she giggled.

"Taxi or walk?" Kieran enquired.

"It's a nice night," she answered. "Let's walk. Three miles won't take long — and it'll be all romantic and eerie along the dark lanes."

"Yeah," Kieran murmured as she snuggled up to him. "Let's hope we don't get lost."

The most arduous part of the walk was the haul up the hill from the sea-front. Once they'd found St Andrew's Road, it was a pleasant stroll in the fresh air. Very little stirred. Occasionally, a car would slice the darkness. Farm animals and rabbits foraged in the fields and by the side of the road. Ali thought she caught the flutter of a bat on its blindfolded hunt for food. Sometimes, a dog would bark briefly and birds hooted. Arm in arm, Kieran and Ali hardly noticed the distance. For once, they had both forgotten murders and mysteries. They concentrated on each other and on the tranquillity. Mostly, they ambled in silence, listening to the spooky sounds of the night.

They turned right by the folk club and followed the valley. There was no pavement so they walked in the narrow road. "Not too far now," Kieran whispered as if it was sacrilege to disturb the subdued pulse of nocturnal life.

"Listen," Ali murmured.

In the valley, an unseen band of crickets took on the role of a rhythm section for the frogs' irregular vocals. Kieran chortled softly. "I heard worse in the club tonight."

Ali stared up at the magical expanse of sky and declared, "There's a lot of stars."

"Don't," Kieran replied. "I always feel so small and insignificant when I think about such things. That's why I live in London. I can cope with mere lumps of concrete. Here, nature's so … big. Overwhelming."

Ali laughed but, seriously, replied, "You'll always be significant to me."

Kieran stopped walking and hugged his girl-friend. "Thanks."

Suddenly, out of nowhere, a car roared down the lane towards them. Its harsh headlights caught them like a pair of petrified rabbits.

Transfixed, Ali yelled, "It's not stopping!"

Still holding Ali, Kieran dived with her into the hedge.

A few seconds later, it was all over. The car was swallowed by the night like a passing ghost. Ali and Kieran picked themselves out of the hedge and brushed themselves down. "That was close," Ali muttered in a quaking voice. "Are you all right? The driver mustn't have seen us – not expecting anyone to be here at this time of night."

"He must have seen us," Kieran grumbled.

"Forget it," Ali said. "No point dwelling on it. Let's just get back to the tent."

The spell had been broken. The rest of the walk seemed dreary and tiring, rather than idyllic and effortless. It was nearly two o'clock when they got to their tent. The site was quiet and unlit. Kieran and Ali stole up to their tent and unzipped the flap slowly so as not to wake the other campers. They clambered inside and closed the fastening again. Ali breathed, "Straight to bed for me."

Kieran agreed. "I'll light the lamp so we can see what we're doing."

He struck a match and turned the valve on the camping gas cylinder. At once, there was an exaggerated hiss of gas. Immediately, a bright yellow flame leapt from Kieran's hand to the canister. There was a loud whoosh and a fireball engulfed the gas cartridge, shot upwards, hit the roof of the tent and spread out in the shape of a mushroom. Kieran felt its heat sear his arm and face. He heard a human scream but did not know if it came from Ali or himself.

A second later, Ali bundled Kieran to the ground and smothered him with a sleeping bag. The tent was in complete darkness. The flash of flame had exhausted itself.

Ali was leaning over him, crying, "Kieran! Kieran! Are you all right?"

Confused, he opened his eyes and saw her silhouette. Tears were streaming down his cheeks but he felt unharmed. He wiped his face with his hand. His eyebrows had disappeared and some of his hair had been singed into short wiry curls. "Yes," he panted. "I'm ... OK. Just shocked, I guess." He sat up, resting on his elbows. He moaned with the effort and then observed, "Phew! There's an awful smell in here."

"It's the gas – and burnt hair," Ali told him. "I'll open the flap."

"The gas control must have been faulty," Kieran surmised.

Letting in some fresh air, Ali remarked, "It's been OK for the last couple of nights." She felt his brow and asked, "Sure you're all right?"

"Yes, I think so."

"We're very lucky, you know. We could've both been killed. The canister didn't have much gas left. And there's not enough air in here to keep a fire going. If the tent had caught, or the bedding ..." She sighed. Holding Kieran, she stammered, "Someone could have sabotaged it while we weren't here. Maybe whoever was driving that car." Chilled, she added, "I'm beginning to think there's something in your hunch, Kieran. Whenever Rhia or this Sandra Jackson go off on holiday, people have a habit of dying."

Kieran nodded. "I know. First, the car. Now this. I get the feeling someone's trying to scare us off. I think we could be in danger."

In shared misery and exhaustion, they keeled over and fell asleep in each other's arms.

10

A li blinked and shifted her position. It was light. She yawned and stretched. Undoing the first few centimetres of the zip, she peered out of the tent into the campsite. It was late in the morning because there was plenty of activity in the field. She closed the flap and watched Kieran. He stirred, let out a long moan, and opened his eyes. "Awake?" Ali asked.

"Mmm. Sort of."

By daylight, Ali assessed the damage. The back of Kieran's right hand was smooth, totally devoid of its down. The hair over his forehead had become frizzled and its nauseating smell still lingered. "You'd better wash it," Ali commented, "or no one will want to come near you." His face was bright red. She touched his cheek. "Does it hurt?"

"A bit," Kieran mumbled. "The only person who can get sunburn at two in the morning."

Ali tried a smile but it wasn't very convincing. She surveyed the tent. The gas light was blackened and its glass guard had shattered. Above it, there was a black mark in the ridge of the tent. The fireball had left dark streaks across the roof where it had scorched the fabric. The tops of the fibre glass poles at each end of the tent also had a thin layer of soot. Ali sighed. "You know when you wake up from a really horrible dream – a nightmare – and suddenly realize that it was just a dream, and there's nothing to worry about after all? Well," she said, "we've just done the same thing in reverse. My dreams were fine but real life … I've woken up to find it's a nightmare."

Kieran sat upright, bearing an expression of sympathy.

"I feel vulnerable in here," she continued. "It's not like bricks and mortar."

"I'll get breakfast," Kieran said, "then we'll talk about it."

"Careful, Kieran. Check the cooker first. I don't want to get paranoid about it but we don't know if anything else has been rigged up to kill us."

It was a pleasant day with a warm breeze. They sat outside on the grass, sipping black coffee and eating cereal. Ali began, "Someone's after us."

"Which means we're on to something," Kieran put in.

"Yes, but who is it?"

"I'll give you two guesses," said Kieran.

"Rhia or Sandra Jackson."

"Spot on, I reckon." He swigged back the dregs of his coffee and got up. "Time to find out which," he declared.

"How?" Ali queried.

Kieran extracted a telephone card from his wallet and waved it in the air. "I call home," he explained. "The camp office has got a phone. Won't be long." He jogged to the reception near the entrance gate.

Three minutes later, he jogged back again, unable to disguise the fact that his plan had worked. He plonked himself down on the grass and reported, "Well, it's not Rhia. She's at home because she answered the phone."

"You just hung up? You didn't say anything?"

"That's right," he answered. "My guess is, she contacted the ferry people and found we were coming to Guernsey. Then she told Sandra Jackson. Immediately, Sandra faked a holiday. She's not really in London – she's still here somewhere. Rhia must have told her which boat we were on. I bet she was waiting for us at the harbour, skulking around somewhere out of view. Followed us to here so she knew exactly where we were. That's how come she could sabotage the lantern last night – and try to run us down when she saw us in the lane."

Ali nodded. "Sandra Jackson," she groaned under her breath. Her distraught expression suggested that she believed her boyfriend's reasoning. "It means we've got to pack up and move on," she concluded. "Find another campsite to disappear into. Stop her finding us for three days. Then we go home."

"Mmm." Kieran thought about it for a moment and then countered, "You know what they say's the best form of defence?"

"Attack? What do you mean?"

"Tonight, I'd like to take a look inside Sandra Jackson's cottage. She's obviously not there, so why not?"

"Because it's breaking and entering!" Ali cried. "It's against the law."

"I think last night's events condone it."

Ali looked up at the sky as if seeking patience or courage. "I know how you feel," she said, "but…"

"How about a compromise?" Kieran suggested. "We pack up here and sneak into a new campsite in the hope that we'll lose her. Then, tonight, we'll try our luck at the bungalow."

Reluctantly, Ali murmured her agreement.

"We'd better buy a torch for the occasion," Kieran added.

Ali nodded and requested, "Make it batteries this time. No more gas, please."

* * *

The first campsite that they tried was full but they got a pitch in Torteval. It was three miles further out of St Peter Port, but they were next to the main road to the airport and the town so it had a good bus service. Anyway, they discovered that they could hire cycles from the campsite office. They gained freedom to ride anywhere at any time.

They found it impossible to enjoy the day. They were too aware that Sandra could be stalking them. Even when they were erecting the tent, they stopped and looked round nervously at each unfamiliar sound. They scrutinized the faces of everyone who came close. Ali was too anxious about Kieran's plans for the evening to relax in the afternoon. They trudged along part of the South Coast Walk, a cliff path, but they did not really appreciate it because it reminded them of their frailty. It would be easy for someone to push them over, down on to the rocks below where the waves crashed pitilessly.

Ali dreaded dusk and the start of their illicit investigation but, in another way, she welcomed it. Like a visit to the dentist with a relentless tooth-ache, she hoped that she would feel better once it was all over.

It was a cool airy evening. The wind came off the sea so, as they cycled along the south road, it blew across them. At midnight there were few cars and they could cycle side by side. Arriving at Jerbourg

Road, they alighted, locked their cycles together behind a hedge, and walked the last hundred metres to Sandra Jackson's cottage. Their hearts pounded but it had nothing to do with the ride.

They did not linger at the front of her bungalow but crept directly to the back. "I hope no one saw us," Ali whispered.

Kieran glanced round. "Everyone's asleep," he assured her. The cottage was empty. There were no lights and the curtains were not drawn. Kieran tried the back door but it was locked. Next he checked out the old sash windows. The one into the spare bedroom was decidedly insecure. It was loose and the wood was rotten in places. He stumbled around the garden till he found an abandoned pitchfork. Jamming the prongs into the gap between the sill and the bottom of the window, he levered upwards. The wood of the sill splintered a little, then there was a small crack as the window catch gave way under the pressure. "We're in," he murmured.

As Kieran slid the window up and clambered into the deserted bedroom, Ali grew tense with nerves and guilt. If it had been light, her red face and frightened expression would have given her away. From inside, Kieran breathed, "Do you want to leave it to me and stay on guard here? You don't have to come in."

"No," she insisted. "I don't want to just stand here. I'd be scared stiff. I'm staying with you." She climbed on to the sill and let herself down carefully into the stuffy bedroom.

"The living room first," Kieran decided.

He took the small torch from his pocket. Making sure that he did not shine it towards a window, he led the way into the hall and then into the lounge. It had the musty smell of an unused room. First, he made for the photograph that he had seen before. He picked it up and shone the torch on it. The image did not look quite right. It had been taken a few years ago before Rhia had acquired her current elegance. Her hair was out of place and her clothes ordinary. "Before she married into money," Kieran muttered.

"Anything on the back?" Ali asked, her voice quaking.

He turned it over but there was nothing to see. He put it down again and looked round the room. There did not seem to be anything extraordinary. A small television, magazine rack, a mixture of classical and old sixties cassettes. Cheap and cheerful paintings of St Peter Port decorated the walls. Kieran opened each cupboard quietly and peered into each drawer in turn.

"You know," Ali whispered, "what isn't here is more remarkable than what is."

"How do you mean?"

A car sounded outside and Kieran snapped off the light, even though they were in a back room.

Both of them held their breath but the engine's roar faded away. Ali sighed and answered, "Not even a video by the telly. Doesn't feel right for a video expert. And just one photo of Rhia. None of Sandra Jackson and her husband."

"If she killed him, she wouldn't want any mementoes, would she?"

"I suppose not," Ali murmured. "But... Never mind." As Kieran continued his search, she continued to brood.

"Wow," Kieran muttered as he opened another drawer.

"What?"

"A rifle," he answered.

Ali groaned and perspired even more. "Why's she got a rifle?"

"I dread to think. Perhaps it was her husband's. Perhaps he was once into clay pigeon shooting."

Ali was not convinced. The weapon made her feel even more uneasy.

"Here's something interesting," Kieran hissed as he rummaged in the next drawer down. "Bills, receipts and things." Barely able to contain his excitement, he said, "Here's one from a Weymouth car hire company. She hired a Toyota from the twenty-first to the twenty-fifth of July!"

Ali knelt down beside him. "That *is* interesting," she said into his ear.

Kieran stuffed the invoice into his jacket pocket

and carried on his investigation. "Look, there's a phone bill – all itemized." He shone the torch on it. "Most of the long-distance calls are to my number. And the longest one was a chat with Rhia on the 5th July! She was certainly plotting something with Rhia."

"I think you've just converted me to your theory," Ali murmured. Thoughts of her father's involvement in Stuart's murder faded to almost nothing.

Kieran's heart stopped as he drew out the last item. It was an old photograph with a young man in the foreground. "That's a young William Jackson," he said. "I recognize him from the picture in the newspaper. But..."

Ali interrupted. "Yes. I see her."

In the background, a young Rhia had been captured, peering with admiration at William Jackson.

"I see her," Ali repeated, "but I don't know what it means."

"No," Kieran replied in a stunned hush. "Nor me."

They stood up. Ali said, "I've had enough. We don't want to be here much longer. Let's get going."

"OK," Kieran responded as he pushed the drawer back into position, "but let's take a quick look in her bedroom first. Just in case."

"All right. But turn off the torch because it'll be at the front and a light will be too much of a give-away."

They tiptoed down the hall and pushed open the bedroom door. The curtains were pulled back so that a little moonlight entered the room. As soon as they stepped inside, Ali and Kieran froze. They looked blankly at each other and then back at the bed in case their eyes were deceiving them. They could see that someone was sleeping under the bed-clothes. The slightly fragrant smell suggested that the figure was a woman.

Ali put her hand over her mouth to stop herself crying out and waking the person in the bed.

Both of them backed out of the bedroom slowly and without a sound. In the hall, Ali's natural instinct was to run but Kieran grabbed her arm. "Quietly," he whispered.

Together, they padded down the hall and into the second bedroom. Quickly, and muffling the sound as much as they could, they climbed out of the window. Back out in the fresh air, Kieran pulled down the window again. He did not shut it completely in case it made a noise when it clicked into place.

Still moving stealthily, they walked round the cottage and back to the main road. There, they could contain themselves no longer. They burst into a run. Neither of them felt any relief until they were back on their bikes and cycling away at speed. Even then, Kieran was overwhelmed by embarrassment and Ali by disgrace. "Never again," she vowed.

"My days as policewoman are over."

"Yeah," Kieran muttered. "That was close. All that time we were in there and she could have caught us. Phew! But," he added between deep breaths, "you must admit, we found out some good stuff."

Ali did not answer. She did not want to admit to profiting from something that she knew was wrong.

When they settled down in the tent, neither of them could sleep. Ali had not shaken off her guilt and Kieran's brain was churning over incessantly. "I really didn't think she'd be hiding in her own place," he whispered. "Assuming it was Sandra Jackson, do you think that's how she did in her husband? She was lurking around – so she could do the dirty deed – but somehow persuaded the police she was somewhere else at the same time?"

Uncooperatively, Ali mumbled, "Could be." For the moment, she had lost her appetite for intrigue.

"With so many coincidences between them, maybe Rhia used the same method. Like Mike said all along, she wasn't in France that Saturday – whatever the videos seem to prove. She was in England, doing *her* dirty deed." Kieran paused and then muttered to himself, "But it was Sandra Jackson who hired the Toyota, not Rhia."

The door flapped and the nylon sides billowed uncannily as the sea breeze infiltrated the tent.

"You know," Kieran said in a hush, "I can't help

feeling the answer's staring me in the face – but I can't see it."

Ali turned towards him. "I'll tell you one thing," she muttered. "We're in deeper trouble now. In the morning, she'll know we broke in. She'll see things disturbed. She'll be after us then. We'd better make ourselves scarce till we go home."

"I suppose so," Kieran replied. "But she may not know where we are right now."

"How many campsites are there on Guernsey? It won't take her long to find us."

"We could take a couple of boat trips. Like the one to Sark. She won't find us then. Even if she did, she couldn't do anything to us on a small launch with other passengers."

"Perhaps not," Ali moaned. "But you can bet she'll check which boat we're going home on. We can't do much about that. She'll book a place as well, if she can. Sooner or later," she said in distress, "she'll catch up with us. I wish we knew what she looked like. I'd feel a bit happier if I knew who to watch out for."

"It's all right," Kieran remarked, holding her arm comfortingly, "there's two of us and only one of her. She's outnumbered. She won't be able get us."

"She seems pretty cunning to me," Ali rejoined.

"We're not exactly stupid ourselves," Kieran contended. "We'll have to be careful and crafty as well."

Ali turned over to seek sleep. Kieran pondered on the photograph that showed that Rhia had met William Jackson many years ago. He could not deduce anything from it other than a connection between Rhia and another murder victim. It seemed that the men in her life were dropping like flies. Eventually he lapsed into sleep wondering if he was to be next.

On a map, Sark was a mere dot. In real life, it was a tall solid plateau jutting out of the sea. An hour-glass lump of rock. It consisted of a few houses, hotels and shacks, lots of horses and carriages, cycles, a couple of tractors and no cars at all. Ali and Kieran could almost taste the alien purity of its air.

The crowd of tourists coming from the harbour soon dispersed. Ali and Kieran decided to hire bikes and ride round the island. They headed south. At the neck of the hour-glass, La Coupée, the land fell away sharply on either side of the track. On one side, a steep path zigzagged down to a large sandy beach. On the other, the inaccessible precipice ended in rocks and the sea. They leaned on the rail on La Coupée and watched the few people that had undertaken the difficult trek down to the beach a long way below them.

"I've been thinking," Ali mentioned as she gulped the clean air. "Why do people keep photos of other people in their houses?"

Kieran looked puzzled but answered the question anyway. "Because they're fond of them in some way, I suppose."

"So who do you keep photos of?"

"Friends and family. What are you getting at?"

A yacht and a small motorboat came into view. The yacht was sailing straight past the island and would soon disappear behind the ragged cliffs that bordered the beach. The launch swung into the calmer waters of the bay. A few tourists walked past Kieran and Ali on the precarious narrow track. Ali and Kieran both turned and examined them, expecting the worst. It was a perfectly normal family and not a psychopathic killer.

Once the family was out of earshot, Ali continued, "Just bear with me. Think of your own house. How many of the framed photos out on show are of friends?"

Kieran thought about it. "Now you mention it, none. They're all family photos, I think."

"Same in my house," Ali remarked. "The ones on display are mainly me, Mum and Dad. There's one of Grandma and Grandad on my mum's side. That's about it."

Out in the bay, the boat dropped anchor. The scream of a hungry baby on the beach drifted up the headland.

Kieran nodded slowly. "I think I see what you're

saying. You think, because of that photo in Sandra Jackson's place, she's related to Rhia?"

"Exactly," Ali uttered.

Kieran exhaled. "Sandra Jackson's part of the family?" He hesitated and then argued, "I doubt it. Remember the newspaper article on William Jackson's murder? It said he was forty-five. If Sandra Jackson's much the same age – which is likely – that's more or less the same as Rhia. But in Rhia's family tree, there's no one who'd be the same age as her. It can't be right."

Ali glanced at her boyfriend and shrugged. "Oh well, it was an idea. You'd better start thinking why else Sandra Jackson might keep a photo of Rhia, then."

Somewhere, there was a bang followed by a thud in the rock below them.

"What was that?" Ali asked.

"Sounded like a car backfiring," Kieran replied.

Ali stared at him and exclaimed, "There aren't any cars on Sark!"

It happened again and a few centimetres from Kieran's hand, something twanged against the rail, making a dent in it.

Kieran grabbed Ali's hand and yelled, "Run!"

They dashed back along the track till they were hidden behind the rocks that rose up on either side. They propped themselves against the rock until they got their breath back.

"Someone was taking pot-shots at us!" Kieran cried. "Probably from that boat."

"And I can guess which rifle was doing the shooting," Ali gasped.

From behind the wall of rock there was the sound of a motor starting up. Kieran walked back up the track until he could see over the bank. "Careful!" Ali shouted.

"It's all right," Kieran called back. "Come and look. The boat's heading back to Guernsey. She's given up."

An old man, wandering along the path, scowled first at Kieran and then at Ali. Still grimacing, he lengthened his stride to get past them faster.

Kieran put his arm round Ali's shoulder and together they watched the launch until it disappeared from view. "Sandra Jackson won't find us on Sark, you said. We'll be safe," Ali mumbled. She wasn't angry with Kieran. She was afraid.

"She must have guessed our tactics," Kieran reasoned. "She must have been keeping watch on the harbour and spotted us this morning. Still, we're safe for now, though. We've just seen her retreat. We can enjoy the rest of the trip."

"Yes, but what about when we get back? She'll be waiting."

Kieran answered, "Maybe. But remember, according to that neighbour, she's supposed to be in England. We know she's only pretending – she's still here — so she won't risk being seen *too* much or she'd blow her cover, as they say. It's one thing to keep a discreet eye on the harbour but it's another to actually do something to us in St Peter Port. Too many people about. All we have to do is make sure we're not followed when we cycle back to the tent. That's easy." He tried to sound certain to give Ali strength and confidence.

"Oh yes?"

"The roads are busy, right? We wait till the traffic comes to a complete standstill and then we ride through it as fast as we can and away. In a car, she'll be stuck."

Ali sighed but seemed reassured by his words. "All right. But don't you think it's time we went to the police?"

"With what?" Kieran asked, clearly doubting the wisdom of her proposal.

Ali shrugged. "Well, you've got that car rental thing."

"Yes," Kieran admitted, "but hiring a car in Weymouth isn't against the law. We've only got theories. Outlandish ones, the police will think. And we still don't know how they did it. There's nothing to back up the video fixing idea."

Ali accepted his argument. They would seem like a couple of hysterical, imaginative kids.

They trudged back to where their bikes lay by the side of the track. "Follow me," Kieran chirped, still trying to cheer her up. "We'll aim for something called the Venus Pool. The guide says it's a natural swimming pool in the rocks at the end of the island. We can relax a bit there."

They spent their last full day in the vicinity of the campsite, biding time, keeping out of Sandra Jackson's way. On the following morning they returned their cycles, packed up the tent and caught the number 14 bus into St Peter Port. The nearer they approached the town, the more edgy they became. Kieran was still trying to convince himself and Ali that, even if Sandra Jackson saw them at the harbour, she would not be able to harm them. With plenty of on-lookers, it would be too chancy for her.

They made sure that they waited for the catamaran where there were lots of other people. A café full of witnesses. When the boarding began, Kieran and Ali first surveyed the territory and then sprinted across the road to join the queue in the ferry terminal. They felt protected by the long line of passengers.

On the boat they took two seats at the back of the lounge so that they could see everything happening in front of them and so that no one could creep up unseen behind them. When Ali grasped his arm, Kieran enquired, "Glad to be going home?"

"You bet," she responded. "But I'm worried in

case she's on the boat with us." She glanced round and mumbled, "She could be anyone."

"She can't do anything here – as long as we don't ask for it by leaning over the rails once it gets going."

Ali smiled weakly. "Wild horses won't drag me on to the deck."

Once the catamaran was skimming across the sea, Ali left her seat only to visit the toilet. She was making her way back to Kieran when she caught sight of a mother struggling with her two young toddlers who had both decided to have tantrums at the same time. For some reason, quite involuntarily, Ali halted to observe the rumpus for a while. As the woman muttered and cursed more heatedly, the kids seemed to enjoy making her life yet more awkward and embarrassing. At first, Ali did not see the significance of the family feud. She didn't understand the impulse that made her linger and watch. A plastic frog hurtled across the gangway and landed at Ali's feet. She bent down and picked it up. Taking it to the harassed mother, she knelt down beside her and shook it in front of the toddler who had thrown it. It rattled pleasingly. The child snatched it back and the mother said, "Thanks."

"They're a handful," Ali remarked.

"You could say that." As Ali stood up, the woman advised her, "Never have two at once!"

While Ali smiled sympathetically at her, the flying frog thwacked into the side of her head.

The mother screeched, "Gemma! That was naughty!"

Ali said, "Never mind," and rushed away.

Kieran rose when she approached. "Are you all right?" he asked anxiously. "You've been a while – and you look like you've seen a ghost."

"Sit down," she ordered, plonking herself back into the chair. "Sit down and listen." She grabbed his arm and shook it in agitation. "It's obvious. You said the answer's been staring us in the face. You were right."

"What are you talking about?"

"A couple of days back, you said it was almost as if Rhia had a double life. Rhia and Sandra could be the same person, you thought, but really you knew they couldn't be. You weren't far out, though. The real answer explains everything – the photos in Sandra Jackson's cottage. The French videos. The car hire in Weymouth. Mike's sighting. It all makes sense!"

Frustrated, Kieran uttered, "What does? You haven't told me yet!"

"You were right all the time, Kieran. Rhia did kill your dad. But she hasn't got a double life – she's got a double!"

"A what?"

"A twin," Ali explained. "Rhia and Sandra are identical twins! It's obvious. Those photos in Sandra Jackson's house weren't of friends *or* family.

They were Sandra Jackson herself – on her own and with her husband."

Kieran's eyes were bright as he nodded. Infected by her excitement, he said, "Yes, of course. The two of them fooled us all. The police videos showed Sandra masquerading as Rhia."

"That's right," Ali replied. "I'm sorry I doubted you about the dress. Rhia didn't have that green dress because she wasn't the woman in the green dress."

"And Rhia gave Sandra a pay-off of one hundred thousand pounds for posing in front of the cameras at the time they'd arranged – when Rhia left her hiding place, went home and murdered Dad. That's why she left evidence of the exact time of the murder and why the only fingerprints on the knife were Rhia's," Kieran concluded. "Sandra came over to England, hired the car, met up with Rhia and took her passport and tickets, I guess. Rhia took Sandra's driving licence and the hire car. It was Sandra Jackson flying from Heathrow, pretending to be Rhia. When she got back, they'd have exchanged documents again and Sandra would have travelled back to Guernsey. Neat. Really, they just swapped places for a few days!"

"Bet it was the second time they'd pulled that trick," Ali added. "Remember Mr Jackson's murder? Sandra had an alibi. The newspaper said she was in Britain. My guess is that she seemed to be on video in Edinburgh at the time. That would have been Rhia's pre-Christmas trip. Actually, Sandra never left Guernsey. She was holed up somewhere on the island, on hand to poison her husband." Abruptly, Ali's flow came to a halt. Disappointed, she spotted the flaw in her own logic. "But she didn't have any medical knowledge. She wouldn't have known enough about drugs to kill him like that."

"No," Kieran put in. "But Rhia would. Ages ago, she was a nurse. She told me. She could have got her sister the pills and given her instructions – as well as an alibi."

"Yes!" Ali was breathless with her discovery and conclusions. She slumped in the chair, almost exhausted.

"Trouble is," Kieran said, "I don't know how we prove it. You must admit, it's clever. They've got a good double act, providing one another with perfect alibis."

"Yes, but at least it means we'll be safe from them here on the boat," Ali estimated. "You were right. Before we left home, Rhia must have phoned Sandra Jackson and told her we were on our way. From that moment, Rhia stayed around London, seeing friends to provide her own alibi and, no doubt, getting herself on video at some London tourist spots for Sandra's alibi. That would have left Sandra in the clear if she had got us on Guernsey.

She wouldn't follow us on to the catamaran, though, because it would take her too close to Rhia. Their little scam is only convincing if they're in different countries."

Kieran nodded but did not reply. He did not wish to scare Ali with his thoughts. He was wondering if Rhia would pretend to be away when they returned. He wondered if Rhia and Sandra Jackson were planning it right now. Rhia could buy a ticket to Guernsey and tell everyone that she was visiting the Channel Islands. Then she would hide out somewhere, ready to pounce on Kieran and Ali. On Guernsey, Sandra Jackson would apparently return from her own phoney trip to London and make herself visible at the exact time that Rhia swooped. The thrill of solving the puzzle gave way to gloom.

"I know why Rhia never mentioned her twin," Ali added. "If anyone else knew she existed, the alibi wouldn't work. But how come she kept it secret for so many years? She couldn't have plotted all this from birth."

"No," Kieran replied. "She's fascinated by genealogy or whatever it's called – her family tree and all that – but Sandra Jackson doesn't appear on it. Strange."

11

The catamaran glided sedately up to Weymouth's harbour wall and the workers on the quay secured the craft with ropes. Customers with cars hurried to the vehicle deck, hoping not to be the last passenger to spill out on to the crowded and narrow streets of Weymouth. Ali and Kieran joined the line of travellers waiting to disembark via the walkway. Ali whispered, "You know as soon as we set foot on dry land we're back in danger, don't you? Rhia this time, not Sandra."

"Yes," Kieran answered. "I know. I've been thinking. There's something I want to do before we get out into the big wide world and face her, though."

"Oh?"

"A telephone call might be interesting."

Before Ali could query further, the queue shuffled forward.

Once on solid ground in the terminal, Kieran made for one in a row of telephones. First, using Directory Enquiries, he found the number of the Guernsey police headquarters in St Peter Port. Then he called the station and asked for the officer in charge of the William Jackson case. When, after a couple of minutes, a female voice came on the line, he stressed, "I need to speak to whoever's heading the investigation into William Jackson's murder."

"And so you are," she replied sharply.

"Oh. Right. Well ... I don't know what you've found out but I imagine Sandra Jackson's alibi was being in Edinburgh. And I guess you've got videos from security cameras to prove it."

There was a barely noticeable pause before the detective said, "Who is this?"

"I can't tell you that yet, but am I right?"

"Yes," she replied cautiously. "But that information was never released. How did you know?"

"Because I'm ... acquainted with her identical twin sister who was in Edinburgh just before last Christmas."

This time, there was a stunned silence. Before the police officer had worked out all of the implications and could ask another question, Kieran hung up. "Yes!" he said, fisting the air. "You were right. Rhia *did* provide a Scottish alibi – just like Sandra

Jackson came up with a French one for Rhia."

Kieran soon sobered up. He was going home to a killer who wanted him dead. As he ambled with Ali towards the exit, he said, "I just hope that the Guernsey police take Sandra Jackson in for questioning now. She can hardly carry out any plan for Rhia if she's in the nick."

Ali stopped and stated, "It won't make any difference to us – or to Rhia. She's just as dangerous because she won't know about it. It's only *after* she's ... you know ... got rid of us that she'll find her alibi's collapsed."

"We'll be OK," Kieran responded. "Just that we've got to plan for ... every eventuality. Come on," he urged. "Let's crack on – and get on with our lives."

In their week away, they had become accustomed to the clean air of the Channel Islands. As they emerged from the terminal, they could sense England's atmosphere of dilute exhaust fumes. Kieran took a deep breath and said, "Smell that? We're home!"

"We're from London," Ali rejoined. "I'll give us two minutes and we won't even notice the pollution any more. You don't when you're in it all the time."

Simultaneously, they froze. "Talking of pollution..." Kieran mumbled. In front of them, standing by a Toyota, Rhia was waving at them to attract their attention.

"Oh, no," Ali groaned.

Thinking quickly, Kieran turned to a lad standing next to him. He was athletic, about thirteen years of age. "You've got broad shoulders on you," Kieran commented. "Bet you'd make a good swimmer."

The boy was wary but smiled at Kieran's flattery. "Already am," he boasted. "Junior champ, me."

"Yeah?" Kieran replied. "That's impressive. What stroke and distance?"

"Hundred metres breast-stroke."

"I bet you're good with numbers, names and faces as well."

"Not bad," the boy mumbled.

"Do me a favour, then," Kieran said to him. "Remember me, Kieran Burrage, and Ali Tankersley here. And remember that lady over there by the car. Her name's Sandra Jackson and she's from Guernsey. Most of all, remember her car's registration. Can you see it?"

The boy was bemused but nodded anyway. He recited the registration for Kieran's benefit.

"Good. If anything happens to us, if you see it on the news or in the papers, go and tell the police that she picked us up and tell them her car's number plate. Will you do that for me?"

The lad shrugged and said, "All right."

Kieran slapped him on the shoulder. "Thanks. And keep up the swimming."

As they continued to walk slowly towards Rhia,

Ali whispered fearfully, "Planning for the worst again, I note. I hope it doesn't come to that. But you could have told him who she really is."

"Perhaps," he answered. "But if I did, Thompson would check who's hired the car, probably find it was someone called Sandra Jackson, and assume that the kid's messing about. End of the line. My way," Kieran explained, "that lad's story and the car rental would match. If the boy remembers the bit about Guernsey, Thompson would have it on a plate."

"Even if you're right that Rhia's used Sandra Jackson's name and licence to hire the car, the trail would only lead to Sandra Jackson. Rhia's off the hook."

Kieran glanced at her and replied, "I don't think so. How strong do you reckon sisterly loyalty is? Do you think Sandra Jackson will take the blame for murders she didn't commit? There'll be no honour between these two, I bet. One will take the other one down with her." There was another reason why he'd refused to name Rhia for the second time in a few minutes. Some instinct told him that he should confront her himself, before he informed the police. It was his right and his duty.

Rhia looked impeccable, like porcelain, and inno-cent. It was impossible to believe that she could be involved in anything sordid. Yet Kieran and Ali had to believe the impossible, because they knew.

Beaming at them like a delighted mother, Rhia chirped, "Hi! Welcome back."

Neither Kieran nor Ali could reply. They just stood there foolishly with their mouths open.

"I checked with the ferry company when you were returning," she explained. "I thought I'd meet you off the boat and give you a lift home. I knew you'd appreciate it. For such a big occasion, I wanted a more ... comfortable car, but this will have to do. Still, it's much more friendly than a coach or train."

"Not the Mercedes, then?" Kieran said pointedly, his tone ringing with sarcasm.

"No," she answered sweetly. "It's being serviced."

Really, Kieran thought, right now she doesn't want to be seen in a car registered in her own name. He shivered.

"Get in," she invited them politely. "I'm dying to hear if you've had a nice time."

Any passers-by would have taken her to be a bubbly parent who had been separated for too long from her loved ones. Presumably, that's why she put on the performance – to convince witnesses that all was well.

Still dumbstruck, Ali and Kieran stood inert on the pavement as she opened the passenger doors for them. "Ali can keep me company in the front," she chimed. "Kieran, you can sit in the back."

Ali clung to Kieran's arm, refusing to budge.

"We'd like to sit together in the back," Kieran declared.

Rhia's mood changed. "No," she barked. "I told you the seating arrangements. Don't make a fuss." Deliberately, she put her hand into her jacket pocket, gripped something inside, thrust it towards Ali, and motioned towards the car's front door.

Kieran groaned. "I think we'd better do what she's suggested," he said to Ali.

The bulge in her pocket could have been a packet of sweets, a pen, almost anything, but Kieran thought that it really was a gun.

Kieran took Ali's rucksack, ushered her, visibly shaking, into the front seat and closed the door. He shoved both bags to the far side of the rear seat and then slipped into the remaining space himself. Leaning forward, he whispered to Ali, "No real choice. It'll be all right. Don't worry."

He looked back towards the ferry terminal and noted with relief that the young swimmer had taken him seriously. The boy was watching every move.

Rhia got into the driver's seat and started the car. It purred into life. Before she pulled away, she said, "Now, let's not have an unpleasant journey. And remember, Kieran, it would be ... unwise to try anything silly when your precious girlfriend is next to me." With one hand on the driving wheel, she tapped the pocket containing the gun to show that, even when she was driving, she could threaten Ali quickly and easily.

"Charming!" Ali cried. "And to think I was the one who tried to persuade Kieran that you were as pure as snow."

"I think you two might have the wrong end of the stick," Rhia responded. "You appear to be assuming my guilt – without a sliver of evidence, I suspect."

From the back seat, Kieran put in, "Are you speaking as Rhia Burrage or Sandra Jackson now?"

"Sandra Jackson?"

"Come on," Kieran blurted out. "Your twin sister must have been on the phone about us. That's why you arranged this little reception, no doubt."

Rhia braked as some traffic lights turned to red. "Twin sister?" she said, twisting round in her seat. "Can you prove that?"

"No, but we know she is. And I've just called the Guernsey police to tell them that she's got an identical twin. I think they'll find that ... interesting. They might begin to question the value of her alibi of being on video in Edinburgh. They might think it's worthy of further investigation."

"You're bluffing," Rhia murmured.

"He's not," Ali emphasized.

"The lights have changed," Kieran prompted her.

Rhia accelerated away from the town towards the A31 and the M3 motorway to London, muttering, "It doesn't make any difference."

Kieran leaned forward. Watching him in the rear-view mirror, Rhia tensed immediately and her right hand dived into her pocket. "I just wanted to ask something," he murmured.

"What?" she snapped, her hand still lingering near the gun.

"It's the only thing we don't understand. How come you kept your twin a secret all these years?"

Rhia sneered. "It wasn't me that kept it secret. It was Father." Abandoning any thoughts of denying that Sandra Jackson was her sister, Rhia decided that she might as well satisfy their curiosity. "Mother died when I was born," she declared, as if she had a divine right to sympathy. "I was brought up by Father. He died last summer, as you know. Just before he passed away, he told me something. He told me that I had a twin sister. He'd kept it from me until the very last moment, too ashamed to admit that he hadn't been able to cope with both babies and so he'd abandoned one. Sandra was adopted." She sighed heavily and with irony. "Funny. I'd always felt there was something missing from my life. Not just a mother. Something else. I tried to make up for it, I suppose, by working out my family tree. For me, it was like a religious calling. But I still didn't feel ... fulfilled. It gave me some experience at tracking people down, though. When Father told me I had a sister, I knew I had to find her straight away. First, I traced the family that had adopted her and then I found Sandra herself. It wasn't easy. Her adoptive family hadn't told her about me, either. She thought they were her real parents. I think Father and the people who adopted her must have made a pact to keep silent."

"That makes sense," Kieran muttered. "When you found her, you worked out a plot to get rid of each other's husbands," he surmised. "And that required you to keep her a secret."

"You make it sound ... cold and calculated," Rhia objected. "But you don't understand. You don't know what it was like. Sandra's life was dreadful, stagnant, held back by poverty and an awful, oppressive husband. He was disabled. Everything she did, she did it for him. Together we decided it was time she had her own life. I helped her to get rid of the shackles. That's all."

"That *is* cold and calculating," Ali retorted.

Before Rhia could turn on Ali, Kieran said, "No doubt you painted a certain picture of Dad for her, as well. To get her co-operation, you probably presented him as some sort of monster."

"If I painted a picture of him, it was accurate. Sandra was more concerned that, if I were free of your dad, I'd be able to help her financially so that her new life would be ... comfortable."

"So," Kieran concluded, "this was the deal. You posed as Sandra in Edinburgh while she murdered an overbearing husband – after you'd sorted out the drugs. In return, plus a hundred thousand pounds, she agreed to stand in for you in Paris, allowing you to kill Dad and inherit a lot of money."

"You *have* been doing some research," Rhia replied.

"It stinks!" Kieran growled.

"All I know is that I've saved my sister," Rhia maintained. "Now, she can look forward to a real life. As long as you two don't spoil it for her. And there's only one way I know that will ensure you don't make nuisances of yourselves…"

"What do you mean?" Ali cried.

Kieran muttered, "She's thinking of removing a threat and getting even more money for herself – by getting rid of me."

"You are cynical, Kieran," his stepmother responded coolly. "I'm not thinking of myself, only Sandra."

"Sure," Kieran uttered. "And I'm second in line for the throne."

Ali murmured, "You won't get away with it."

Rhia glanced at her watch and then announced, "Look, this is the New Forest. It's a lovely place. We'll take a detour somewhere – to see more of it."

Ali glanced back at Kieran. Her expression suggested alarm. Both of them knew that Rhia was plotting more than simple sightseeing.

She turned left on to a track that led deep into the

woodland. "There's a gorgeous place up here," she informed them.

"And what have you got in mind?" Kieran barked.

"A break in the journey. A bit of relaxation," she lied.

Kieran did not persist in his questioning. He had a good idea what was on her mind. He had to wait until he had an opportunity to strike back.

She drove carefully along the pot-holed trail until she pulled into a secluded parking place. The car was hidden by a screen of ancient trees.

"Let's get out," she said. Her tone fell somewhere between a command and a suggestion. "There's a beautiful spot just through these trees. Bring your backpacks."

Kieran and Ali looked at each other anxiously but obeyed.

Well away from the main road and with the car engine off, there was a deadly calm. Only the birds among the upper branches went about their business, uncaring of the feud between three insignificant human beings.

"You'll love it," Rhia announced, as she took a heavy bag from the boot.

Standing side by side for protection in the dense forest, Kieran and Ali shuddered. Neither of them moved.

There was no pretence any more. Rhia yanked

the gun from her pocket and waved it in the direction that she wanted them to go. "Some people have to be encouraged to enjoy themselves," she observed.

Kieran took Ali's hand and set off among the trees. There was no path but the comings and goings of squirrels and ponies had kept the way clear. Immediately, he had to let go of Ali because there was not enough room for two abreast. After just a few seconds of walking, trees surrounded them, isolating them utterly from the rest of the world. They were trapped in a murky microcosm of their own with a murderer. Without Rhia it would have been a pleasing screen from prying people. With her, it was claustrophobic and menacing.

As they trekked into the forest, they became aware of the sound of running water. Shortly after, the trees thinned a little and a river appeared in front of them. Really it was only a stream but, at this point, there was a bend in its course and erosion had widened it. Nearer to the inner bank, the water was slack and inviting. Kieran and Ali halted. Rhia had been right. It was lavish and lonely, like a natural temple encircled with trees. To either side of the curve, both upstream and downstream, the trees grew impenetrably right down to the banks so a riverside walk was impossible. Rhia leaned against a trunk, put down the bag and said, "You can make camp here."

"What?" Kieran exclaimed.

"Packs off," she ordered. "Pitch your tent by the river. It's a super place for it."

Kieran sighed. He remembered that, several years ago, he envisaged Rhia as a sharpshooting stranger imposing herself on the Burrages. He did not realize how accurate the image would turn out to be. Rhia was propped against the tree, gun in hand, as if she were in a wild west saloon, expecting trouble.

Dragging the folded tent out of Ali's rucksack, Kieran tried to work out the cruel plan that was in his stepmother's brain. "What are you trying to set up here?" he murmured, not expecting a reply. "We got back from Guernsey, perhaps out of money. No coach or train fare. Maybe we hitched a lift this far – found this remote spot and decided to camp overnight." As they assembled the poles, Kieran deduced, "You're setting up some sort of accident! Just in case. I bet in Weymouth you bought a ticket for the ferry but didn't use it. That way, the travel company's registered that you're in Guernsey. You've probably got Sandra working on an alibi right now."

Rhia was smirking. She checked the time as if to confirm that she was working to an agreed schedule.

Kieran continued. "Really, you could kill us any-how – you could just shoot us – but you're making it look like some accident in case the alibi doesn't hold up, in case the police *are* on to Sandra. Besides, you don't want to overuse the twin sister trick. This way – manufacturing an accident – you may not need her to double for you."

Ali had stopped helping to erect the tent and was staring at Kieran, hoping that his horrifying logic was the product of a warped and hyperactive imagination. The sight of Rhia toying with a pistol dismissed any hope that he was mistaken. She shook her head and fought to keep back tears. She was determined not to show her weakness in front of Rhia. Ali was praying that Kieran had a plan to get them out of trouble – or that something would occur to her. Really, she wanted to collapse inside the still sagging tent, hide, cry, and only emerge when it was safe – when her world had righted itself and, unharmed, she could carry on her normal, uneventful, carefree life.

Slowly, Kieran lapped the site, tightening the guy ropes, pulling the tent into shape. When he'd finished, Rhia called, "Well done. Now spread out your things inside as if you were staying overnight. Keep the flap open so I can see." She moved into a position where she could keep an eye on them.

Inside, manhandling the sleeping bags, Ali whispered to Kieran, "She's going to kill us! What are we going to do?"

"Wait to see what she's got in mind," he breathed. "Wait for an opportunity."

From outside, Rhia's sarcastic voice muttered, "Very cosy."

Kieran and Ali scrambled out and stood, like sentries, either side of the door. They stared at Rhia, awaiting orders.

Rhia glanced once more at her watch. Her smile suggested self-satisfaction. "Now, Ali, you get back in and strip off."

Ali cried, "What? Why?"

"Get into your swimming costume," she commanded, pointing the gun at her to show that she meant it. "As you surmised, Kieran, you've just arrived here, pitched the tent, and, to relax before an evening meal, Ali's decided to take a dip in the river. It could hardly be more attractive for it. But don't think you're being left out," she said to her stepson. "You're going to have a swim as well. You'll keep your clothes on, though."

Kieran responded, "If you've got it in mind to have us drown, it won't look very convincing. You know we're both strong swimmers. Even if one of us had a problem, the other would sort it out."

"I know," Rhia groaned. "Do you think I'm a complete fool?" Once more, she waved the gun at Ali and snapped, "Go on, then, get in and change." To Kieran, she said, "You've decided to have a nice cool drink before joining her." Walking backwards so that she could keep the gun trained on him, she went for the bag.

She returned and put the bag down close to Kieran. Then she backed away from it and told him to extract the contents.

Kieran peered inside and then took out the six cans of beer. He glanced at Rhia suspiciously.

"Take a couple down to the stream and put them in the water to cool them down," she directed him.

While Rhia watched him carefully, he negotiated the bank with two of the cans in his hands. The slope down to the river was gentle and bore the signs of animals. Birds had hopped around and ponies had come to the water for a drink. He placed the cans securely in the stream where the flow was lazy.

"Right," Rhia called. "Back up here. Erecting the tent was thirsty work. You need some refreshment. Drink one of the beers. All of it."

At last, Kieran understood her plan. Ali was to go for a dip while he had a few innocuous drinks. Ali would get into trouble and Kieran would spring into action. But he would be in no fit state to help her. His drunken attempt to save his girlfriend would result only in his own drowning. Two victims rather than one.

He opened the can and gulped some of it down.

"Faster," Rhia demanded.

As Ali clambered out of the tent with one arm behind her back, Kieran finished off the beer.

"Good," Rhia uttered. "Put the empty can by the

door to the tent and then open another."

Kieran scowled at her. Holding his stomach, he muttered, "I can't. I'm all bloated already."

Rhia aimed the gun at his head and cried, "Don't try your luck! Of course you can. Get on with it."

Kieran shrugged, dropped the first can near Ali's feet and then fetched another one. As he bent down and all of Rhia's attention was on him, Ali lifted her arm and threw their peg hammer directly at Rhia.

She was too far away, though. Rhia had the time to side-step. She took the blow on her thigh. "Ow!" she squealed. But the hand that held the weapon did not waver. She cursed Ali but almost immediately she laughed aloud. "What a silly impetuous girl you are," she mocked. "Right. Finish that drink, leave the tin near the last one and bring the other two down to the bank."

She instructed Ali to get into the water and Kieran to sit on the edge of the bank and begin the third beer. Then she called to Ali, "Swim up and down. Enjoy it – like training. I want to see you go fast. You're supposed to be good so show off to me."

Kieran mumbled to himself, "She wants Ali to be tired out before she organizes the drowning! Lower her resistance."

After a while, Kieran could feel the effects of the alcohol. He began to feel detached from the horrible situation that Rhia had set up so efficiently. When he glanced from Ali in the river to Rhia standing further along the bank, his eyes took longer than usual to focus. His stomach was full and queasy.

"Drink!" Rhia yelled at him.

Blinking and lolling, Kieran lifted the can to his lips and gulped yet more of the sickening liquid. His legs dangled from the overhanging edge and swung erratically. He regarded Ali with sympathy and love. In the water, no one could distinguish her tears from river water. She was being punished simply for being with him. This whole affair had nothing to do with her. He had dragged her into it and now she was about to be killed just for being his girlfriend.

Ali reached one end of the pool yet again and stopped momentarily to catch her breath. At once, Rhia barked, "Swim! Faster."

Behind them, beyond the tent, there was a rustling in the undergrowth. Kieran's head twisted round and he fought to bring his eyes to a focus. He was hoping to see the cavalry, charging to the rescue. But it wasn't. It was just a couple of wild ponies approaching the stream.

While Rhia was distracted, Kieran decided to make his move. He scrambled to his feet and began to hurtle towards Rhia. Almost immediately, he slipped and tumbled over. It was a laughable, pathetic attempt. When he looked up towards his stepmother, he saw the barrel of her gun pointed directly at his head. Even if he hadn't been befuddled, he would not have been able to take her by surprise. The decoy was feeble and the distance too great. Rhia sniggered and the ponies retreated into the forest.

"Excellent," Rhia declared. "The alcohol is getting to you. To show such recklessness – and bad judgement – you must be nearly ready. Finish off the last pint."

Kieran's grip on reality was becoming ever more slender. He could no longer arouse any worthwhile opposition. He lurched back to his place on the crest of the bank and swallowed the remaining beer in a single draught. In a slurred voice, he pronounced, "Done." It was an admission that he had consumed the drink and that he was helpless.

"Good," Rhia replied. "It's time you joined your girlfriend. Into the river with you."

Kieran obeyed blindly. He stumbled down the bank and waded into the cool water.

Gasping for breath, Ali joined him.

"Now," Rhia said with an ugly grin, "I want you to pick up anything heavy from the bottom."

Kieran stared at her for a few seconds, unable to comprehend. "What for?"

They stood there like fools in the sluggish part of the river, one intoxicated and one exhausted. They clung to each other and tottered together.

"Because you're going to crack her over the head with it – the sort of injury she could have sustained if she'd dived in carelessly."

Even his confused brain registered revulsion at her demand. "No!" he protested.

Rhia grimaced with frustration. "I thought this is where you might draw the line." Keeping the finger of her left hand on the trigger and maintaining her aim, Rhia bent down and picked up a massive bough in her right hand. "I'll do it instead!" Without warning she flung the bough violently at Ali's head.

Intuitively, but still in a daze, Kieran put out his arm to protect Ali. The branch thwacked him painfully and knocked his arm backwards on to Ali. Both of them toppled over.

In the instant that Kieran plunged into the river, the cold water revived him. At once, he could make dreadful sense of their predicament. With his mind cleared, he decided what they had to do. He dragged Ali back up to the surface and whispered to her. "Deep breaths! And get ready to hold one."

Ali had been stunned. In a broken voice, she murmured, "No chance."

"Do it," Kieran dictated. "It's the only way."

Rhia was heading for them with a rock in one hand and her gun in the other.

Kieran positioned himself in front of Ali. "No, Rhia. I won't let you hurt her."

Rhia raised her arm to hurl the rock.

"Now!" Kieran cried. He grabbed Ali's arm, turned and dived out into the rapidly flowing part of the stream as if he were in a vital race. Ali lunged after him. Staying underwater, they swam as best they could and let the river carry them away from her.

Kieran felt the rock thud on to his back but the water stripped it of much of its force. Even submerged, Kieran heard the crack of the gun. There was a ping in the water as the bullet zipped past his head. It wasn't difficult to keep underwater. Kieran's heavy clothes dragged him down. The second bullet sliced through the river and into his leg just above the ankle. He opened his mouth to cry out in agony but instead he choked. He kept going for as long as he could but then he had to fight to reach the surface. Coughing and spluttering, he was amazed and relieved to see Ali still by his side. Her face was red with the effort of holding her breath, but she had surfaced at the same time and was swimming breast-stroke. His plan had worked. He turned on to his back, letting the current complete his escape. Rhia and the curvature of the river were out of sight. "We made it," he called to Ali. "Let's get out here. She got my leg."

They swam across the flow and scrambled out on to the opposite bank. Ali was weak but she helped Kieran hobble on to dry land and behind some trees where they were out of view.

"She won't find us here," Kieran groaned. "There's no path by the river so she can't follow us – and she can't swim." He turned his head to one side, coughed and then vomited until his stomach had rejected all of the beer. He was shivering with cold and shock.

Crashed out in the undergrowth, Ali asked, "Are you OK?"

"Better for being sick," he answered. Gingerly, he pulled up his trouser leg to inspect the damage. Watery blood had seeped down his left leg and into his sock.

"Oh, no," Ali moaned.

"It's not too bad," Kieran assured her. "I think it's gone right through – just under the surface. Too messy to be sure, but I think it looks worse than it is."

"I hope you're right. It looks awful to me."

Kieran rubbed his arm gently. "This isn't too good either. It's where the branch got me."

"I hope it's not broken or anything."

"No," Kieran replied. "Quite a bruise, I should think, but I'll live."

"I'm glad about that." Ali surveyed the wreck of her boyfriend sympathetically. He was trembling, pale and saturated. Slowly recuperating herself, she said, "I hate to say this, but what now? Rhia won't give up, you know. Maybe it'll take her a while, but she'll find us."

"Yes," Kieran agreed. "I think the main road's that way," he said, pointing behind her. "We should head for it and get help."

"Really?" Ali muttered questioningly. "Can you walk that far? And it's exactly what she'll expect, surely. She could be making her way there now – to cut us off."

"True," Kieran admitted. "So what do you suggest?"

Ali shrugged. "I guess we do what she'd least expect us to do."

"What's that?"

"Go back. Go back and look for help in the other direction. That way, we can nip into the tent. You need warm dry clothes."

"But..." Kieran sighed. "You're probably right."

"How's the leg?"

"I think you were right about walking. It's not going to hold up for long."

"There's no way through this wood anyway," Ali said. "How about swimming?"

"Less painful than walking," Kieran estimated. "But how about you? It'd be against the current. Not easy."

Ali tried to raise their spirits. "Remember the four by one hundred relay in Glasgow? I swam the last leg. My best ever. I hit the water in seventh place. By the end of the first length, I was in third. Everyone thought I'd burnt myself out, but I kept going."

"Yes," Kieran murmured. "But ... you didn't win."

"No, but pulling the team from seventh to second was pretty miraculous." She grinned. "I'll make it back upstream. I'm more worried about you. Still, as long as you can swim to the tent, you could rest there while I go for help. That track we drove along must go somewhere in the other direction. I'll give it a try."

Kieran limped back to the stream and gently lowered himself into the cold water. Ali followed him. The current hadn't carried them a great distance but, even so, the return journey was laborious. Without a sound, they swam into the slack water of the bend and stood, breathing hard. The site was deserted. Their orange tent looked lonely and out of place.

Kieran stepped forward and winced with pain. His leg was getting worse. "Let's get you inside and wrapped in something warm," she said, offering her shoulders to lean on.

Together they staggered to the door of the tent, squatted down and unzipped it. Inside, her knees drawn up to her chest, Rhia was sitting and waiting. She was grinning insanely and holding the gun in both hands on top of her knees.

12

"Chasing you was hopeless," Rhia proclaimed. "Besides, I didn't think you'd get far with that wound. I had an inkling you'd double back." She squeezed the trigger.

Ali pushed Kieran one way and leapt the other way herself. The flap of the door closed and then twitched as the bullet pierced it, flew past Ali's ear and slammed into a tree.

Instinctively, as she fell sideways, Ali kicked as hard as she could at the base of the fibreglass pole. The support fell in and the front end of the tent collapsed. Inside, Rhia swore and fired again. The shot ripped through the fabric and screamed harmlessly into the far, eroded bank of the stream.

Ali and Kieran lay low either side of the deflated

tent while Rhia tried to disentangle herself from the nylon. From outside, it looked funny. If it had not been a murderous adult, it could have been some silly kid pretending to be a ghost draped in an orange sheet.

"Quick!" Kieran called to Ali. "Unhook the guy rope on your side. Throw it to me."

Guided by the direction of his voice, Rhia took aim and fired through the material again. Kieran shrieked as the bullet grazed his arm. Ignoring the pain, he caught the rope with his other arm. As quickly as he could, he bound it securely to the peg on his side, trapping Rhia in the bottom half of the tent. She was as good as tied up. But she was still able to fire the weapon. Even if she could not see to aim, she was a threat, like a caged animal. Kieran knew very little about guns but, if films were anything to go by, he calculated that she had one shot left. He crawled away to a different position. In silence, Ali joined him and together they watched Rhia labour like a wasp trying to emerge from its pupa. Ali was cowering and uncertain. Next to her, Kieran shook with cold. He was bleeding from three wounds and light-headed. Neither of them was in a fit state to run away. They were entranced by the strange spectacle of the frenzied creature writhing inside the tent.

Suddenly, their worst fears were realized.

Rhia had got hold of their kitchen knife and used

it angrily to slash through the nylon. From the bottom to the top, the fabric was slit by the sharp blade. And Rhia burst from her cocoon like an enraged demon. She had dropped the gun to cut her way out so she stood there, surrounded by the remnants of the tent like a discarded dress, with the knife in her hand.

With one final effort, Kieran struggled to his feet drunkenly and squared up to his stepmother. "Just like the knife you used on Dad," he commented.

Rhia glanced at it and her lips twisted into a smile. "Yes," she admitted. "And I'm not finished yet."

Kieran stood in front of Ali who was too startled to move from the ground. "Come on, then," Kieran challenged her. "Let's get it over with."

She did not need the invitation. She charged at Kieran like a savage soldier with a thirsty bayonet.

Kieran stood his ground until the very last moment. As she lunged at him, he dodged out of the way. She flashed past him and then screeched as she tumbled over Ali. Her shrill cry turned into a hideous scream when she crashed to the earth. She did not attempt to rise.

Ali, nursing her shin where Rhia had kicked it, peered anxiously at her boyfriend. He returned her look and then they both stared at Rhia, still stricken on the ground. "I think she's ..." Kieran approached her cautiously.

"Careful," Ali muttered fearfully.

He knelt down, a metre away from her. She was sprawled on her side and there was a moist red stain near her stomach but her chest still rose and fell weakly. Her eyes were closed and strange little gasps issued from her mouth. The bloodied knife lay in front of her. Kieran leaned forward and moved it out of her reach. "She's alive," he called to Ali, "but in a bad way."

Ali forced herself upright and staggered towards him. "Get the car key," she suggested. "She put it in her jacket pocket."

Kieran felt like an impatient vulture. Revolted, he picked carefully at her pocket. As he drew out the key, Rhia's eyes flickered open. In a croaky voice, she whispered, "I guess it's all over."

Kieran lowered his gaze as if he were the guilty one. He nodded.

She swallowed and grimaced, clearly suffering from her injury. All trace of her veneer of elegance had been stripped away. She was a wreck – a sad victim of her own making. "I really wanted to help Sandra, you know." She closed her eyes again, coughed and clutched her stomach. "*Did* you tell the police about her?"

Kieran murmured, "Yes."

Rhia sniffed and sighed wearily. "It's over for her as well, then. But, I tell you, the police won't have her. Not Sandra."

Puzzled, Ali and Kieran glanced at each other. "Come on," Ali said, taking his arm and dragging him up. "We've got to get moving. You need help. She needs help, I guess, even if she doesn't deserve it. I've had a couple of lessons so I can probably drive the car."

"It doesn't seem right to leave her like this," Kieran mumbled.

"Go," Rhia interjected. "I want to be on my own."

Kieran shook his head despondently, groaned and then nodded. "OK," he consented.

When the way through the trees was too narrow for Ali to support Kieran, she found him a stout stick to lean on. Slowly, like the wounded returning from war, they shuffled back towards the car. It wasn't far but it seemed like a marathon.

At last they reached it. Kieran rested against the passenger's side of the Toyota while Ali went to the driver's door. Just before she used the key, there was a loud bang from the direction of the river. Birds scattered nervously from the trees. In horror, Ali and Kieran stared at each other over the top of the car. "Oh no!" they uttered together.

Rhia Burrage had used the last bullet on herself.

Ali and Kieran fell into the car and wept with exhaustion and pity. Eventually, Kieran wiped his face and murmured, "Now it *is* all over."

* * *

Separated for most of their lives, unaware of each other, the twins still shared more than their appearance. Both were prepared to kill to liberate themselves from their husbands and neither was able to cope with the thought of a trial for murder. On Guernsey, Sandra Jackson took her husband's rifle, hired a motor launch and set out to sea. First she shot a hole in the boat and then in herself. Both twins found the same way out.

Wanting to kill Stuart Burrage was not an offence but John Evans still faced a charge of attempted murder. Because he had also confessed to a murder that he didn't commit, it was likely that he would be declared unfit to stand trial. He would be treated rather than punished. Ali's father, Robert Tankersley, was made bankrupt by the out-of-court settlement over his infringement of copyright. Ali believed that it made him a better person. No longer did he trade in people's lives.

A few days of rest cured Ali of the physical effects of Rhia's attack. Kieran needed longer but his injuries were not serious. The bone in his arm had been chipped but both bullets caused only flesh wounds that were soon treated in hospital. There was another type of damage. The nightmare of being hunted like animals by Rhia would stay with Ali and Kieran for ever. That scar would never heal.

Not yet fit, Kieran sat in the auditorium and

yelled his support for the team. Ali had already won the 100 metres backstroke and she was about to complete the double by taking the 200 metres race as well. The water rushed past her as she surged down the final length. How could he ever have believed that the current of a river would get the better of her? She touched home a full second before her nearest rival. Standing in the water, she waved triumphantly towards Kieran in the crowd. There was no comparison with the person who had stood in that stream, exhausted and numbed with fright. He cheered her victory.

Afterwards, when they met in the café, he kissed her and murmured, "Great stuff!" When among friends, they had never before shown their affection. They had not tried to hide it. It had simply not been uppermost in their minds. Now, their relationship had been set in stone by sharing and enduring adversity. They became even closer.

Sitting over a glucose drink, Kieran murmured, "You know, I do wonder if it would've been different if I'd tried harder to get on with her."

"Oh, Kieran. I'm not having you think like that," Ali declared. "It had nothing to do with you. Rhia was after your dad's money. Full stop. Even if you'd been her best buddy, she'd still have been after the loot."

"I suppose so," Kieran responded. "I went down to the cemetery today," he whispered, reddening.

"It sounds silly, but I suppose I told Mum all about it."

Ali reached across the table and took his hand. "That's not silly," she replied softly. "Did it help?"

"Yes, I guess so."

"Then it was perfectly sensible." She smiled at him.

With an excited bound, Mike Spruzen arrived at their side. "Just heard!" he bellowed. Addressing Kieran, he babbled, "You were shot twice! Amazing." He grabbed a chair and plonked himself down. "Reminds me of something that happened to me once. You'll understand this now. I was with this girl. Absolute stunner. Film star and supermodel league. Well, as you do, we tried to creep back to her house in the middle of the night, you know." He winked at them. "Trouble was, her old man spotted us. He belted downstairs. 'What do you think you're doing with my daughter?' he yells at me. Then, he pulled this gun out of his dressing gown pocket. Don't know what sort it was. Probably a semi-automatic…"

Unable to maintain straight faces any longer, Ali and Kieran burst out laughing. "Nothing changes!" Ali exclaimed.

With a puzzled expression, Mike uttered, "What's got into you two? It was serious. I could have been topped for that girl."

Ali smiled at him. "Sorry," she said. "We didn't mean to spoil your story. Carry on. We know it's no fun. We had to face just an ordinary gun. It must have been awful if he had something special."

"You're not kidding!" Mike pronounced. "Anyway, I'll tell you how I got out of it. Real cool, I was…"

Ali and Kieran allowed him to outpoint them. His comic-strip adventure was too divorced from reality to offend them. He lived in a parallel fantasy world where it was possible to be cool under fire, where no one got hurt, where endings were always happy.

P●INT CRiME

A murder has been committed . . . Whodunnit?
Was it the teacher, the schoolgirl, or the best friend? An
exciting series of crime novels, with tortuous plots and lots
of suspects, designed to keep the reader guessing till the
very last page.

•PATSY KELLY•
INVESTIGATES

When Patsy starts work at her uncle's detective agency, her instructions are very clear. Do the filing. Answer the phone. Make the tea. *Don't* get involved in any of the cases.

But somehow Patsy can't help getting involved...

And it's not just the cases she has to worry about. There's Billy, too. Will she ever work out what she *really* feels about him...?

•PATSY KELLY•
INVESTIGATES

Anne Cassidy

Look out for:

A Family Affair
End of the Line
No Through Road